# Amelia's Back-to-School Survival Guide

by Marissa Moss
(and get-ready-for-school Amelia)

## FEATURING

**VOTE 4 Amelia** and **Amelia's GUIDE TO BABYSITTING**

DOUBLE THE PREPARATION,
DOUBLE THE SURVIVAL!

SIMON & SCHUSTER BOOKS FOR YOUNG READERS
NEW YORK   LONDON   TORONTO   SYDNEY   NEW DELHI

D0478635

This notebook is dedicated to
Steven Moss—
I'd vote for you!

SIMON & SCHUSTER BOOKS FOR YOUNG READERS
An imprint of Simon & Schuster Children's Publishing Division
1230 Avenue of the Americas, New York, New York 10020
Vote 4 Amelia
Copyright © 2007 by Marissa Moss
Amelia's Guide to Babysitting
Copyright © 2008 by Marissa Moss

SIMON & SCHUSTER BOOKS FOR YOUNG READERS
is a trademark of Simon & Schuster, Inc.
Amelia® and the notebook design are
registered trademarks of Marissa Moss.

For information about special discounts for bulk purchases, please contact Simon & Schuster
Special Sales at 1-866-506-1949 or business@simonandschuster.com.

The Simon & Schuster Speakers Bureau can bring authors to your live event. For more
information or to book an event, contact the Simon & Schuster Speakers Bureau at
1-866-248-3049 or visit our website at www.simonspeakers.com.

A Paula Wiseman Book

Book design by Amelia
(with help from Tom Daly)

My hands
are too tired → The text for this book is hand-lettered.
to face
homework!

Manufactured in China
0212 SCP

2   4   6   8   10   9   7   5   3   1

CIP data for this book is available from
the Library of Congress.

ISBN  978-1-4424-4349-5

These titles were previously published individually

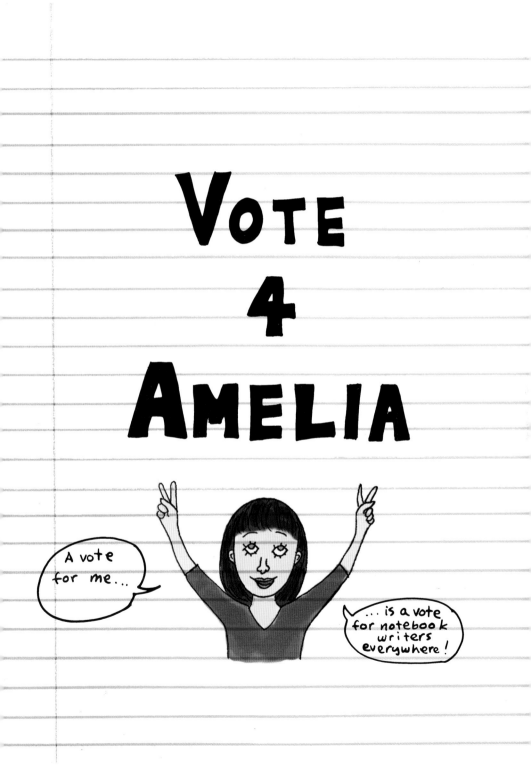

The school is covered with campaign slogans these days. Even bathroom stalls have posters taped on them, urging you to "Vote for Hudson for Prez" or "Vote for Olivia— I'll luv ya 4 it!" Some are pretty sloppy, some use cut-out letters so they look like ransom notes, and some are gorgeous works of art. Those are the ones I made — the beautiful ones.

When Carly decided to run for student body president, she wanted me to be her campaign manager— in other words, make her posters and think up catchy slogans. It's actually kind of fun. I like writing **Carly is Cool!** in big bubble letters. And I thought my dartboard idea was a work of genius. But there's a part that's not so good. Carly wanted me to run <u>with</u> her, so we could be on the Student Council together.

So while she's running for president, I'm running for secretary, and Leah is running for treasurer (the perfect job for her because she's so neat and organized).

The competition for president is fierce because a lot of people want the job, but really Carly only has to worry about one rival — Hudson.

Carly          vs.          Hudson
↓                           ↓

↑
Carly is smart and popular. Kids like and respect her, and everyone knows how passionate she is about public causes after she collected all that money for hurricane victims last month.

↑
I don't know if Hudson is smart or not — it's hard to tell. But he's cute and VERY popular, one of the coolest kids in school, so he really doesn't have to be good at anything.

And me for secretary!
↓

I'm not cool, or popular, but I figure if Carly wins, I will too.

People will think of us together since we're best friends, and when they vote for her, they'll vote for me.

To be a good candidate, you have to be outgoing and energetic. You have to talk to people and make them like you. Those are things I'm _not_ good at. I'm better at behind-the-scenes kind of stuff — like dreaming up ideas for campaign slogans or posters and thinking of ways to make people pay attention to Carly.

Luckily, running for secretary is not exactly a high-profile job. It's not the sort of position people care passionately about. In fact, it's kind of like voting for chief dishwasher or head crosswalk guide. It's just a task _someone_ has to do. There's no glamour to it at all — none.

what does a secretary do anyway? I know they write down the minutes to each Student Council meeting, but is there anything else they do?

↓

I can take down minutes at least — I'm good at writing quickly. →

← Maybe not neatly, but quickly.

arrange things alphabetically? ↓

sharpen pencils? ↓

file folders? ↓

To be president, though, you need ideas — you need a reason people should vote for you, like plans for how you'd make things better at school. Some of the candidates have pretty silly ideas. Olivia promises that if she's elected, every Friday will be pizza day in the cafeteria instead of what it is now — Mystery Mush of Leftovers Day.

I like pizza, but that doesn't solve the leftover mush problem. The hairnet ladies will just make the mush on Thursday instead of Friday.

Carly takes the office of student body president more seriously than that. She has plans, BIG plans. Her number one priority is to take the TV sets in every classroom and put them to good use.

The way the school got the TVs in the first place was kind of sleazy.

Some company gave them to the school, but in return the principal had to agree to broadcast their "news" program once a week.

The problem is, it's not really news — it's more like propaganda with <u>lots</u> of ads to get kids to buy junk food, soda, clothes, shoes, all kinds of stuff no one needs. So we're forced to watch a bunch of ads with the illusion that there's some educational content to the programming.

Carly wants to change all that. She wants the kids in the Media class to use the donated audio-visual equipment to make our <u>own</u> news program, reporting on things that happen at school. I think that's a genius idea!

Of course, Carly wants to be one of the reporters. She'd be great at it!

And that's our story on the top prize winners in the science fair. Congratulations to all the students who worked so hard on their exhibits.

Now, to Luke with sports.

The things the other candidates are promising seem completely unrealistic next to Carly's plans. Eric says he'll make the schoolboard change the schedule so classes start at noon and kids can sleep late.

Of course, everyone loves that idea, but we all know that will never happen.

It makes for a fun campaign, though, even if it isn't realistic. To promote himself, Eric comes to school in pajamas, and his posters promise "No more baggy eyes!" and "Feel rested and learn more!"

bed-head—
he doesn't comb
his
hair →

robe →

slippers →

He's giving away those sleep masks some people use on airplanes.

It's so clever, people might vote for him just because he's packaged himself so well, even though no one believes he can really get the schedule changed.

Cassandra is running for president with the slogan "Vote for the Future." She says she'll get the school to provide everyone with a free laptop computer. All assignments would be submitted electronically, and all textbooks would be on the computers, so there'd be no more heavy backpacks.

If I thought she could really pull it off, even _I_ would vote for her!

Who wouldn't trade a backbreaking load of books for a sleek, ultra-modern, light laptop?

this...          ... or this?

But we all know that will NEVER happen. Who will pay for computers? Who will put all the textbooks into a digital database? When you try to pin her down on those kinds of details, she doesn't have any answers.

The only candidate other than Carly with a realistic plan is Hudson, but it's not a reality I like.

His campaign slogan is "Vote for a Sweeter School – Vote Hudson!" He promises to have vending machines installed all over the school, so kids will never be far from a sugar fix. Since his dad is a Candy-Matic dealer, he can probably actually make this happen, but I don't think that's a good thing. I like candy as much as the next person, but I know it's not good for you.

WARNING: Can cause cavities, sugar highs, and obesity!

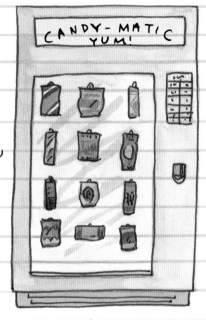

Hudson gives out candy bars to get kids to vote for him. Who can say no to free candy? I have to admit, I almost took one, but then I couldn't face Carly's disappointment, so I didn't.

Carly especially HATES this idea! She doesn't eat junk food herself and makes her mom buy organic groceries, so to her this kind of thing is horrible pollution. Myself, I wouldn't mind one candy machine in the cafeteria, but NOT all over the school.

IF U ♥ CHOCOLATE
VOTE 4 HALLIE
THE CHOCOLATE ♛QUEEN!

↑
She's not promising to give you chocolate, but simply the association of something delicious with her name is supposed to make you want to vote for her.

I WUV U DIS MUCH!

VOTE U-NICE!

Who's → against peace? Nobody! Does it matter that wars aren't topics for school decisions? Of course not! If you're against bad, mean war, you have to like Sandro, don4 you?

the "Aw-how cute!" ↑ factor - who can resist those eyes?

VOTE FOR WORLD PEACE!
VOTE FOR SANDRO!
PRESIDENT FOR PEACE!

# SLOGANS

This is another unrealistic candidate. If it sounds too good to be true, it probably is. He'll still get some votes — I guarantee it!

NO MORE HOMEWORK! VOTE 4 DAN!

TURN SCHOOL INTO **POOL**
OUT WITH DESKS!
IN WITH POOL TABLES!
VOTE 4 CARLOS!

↑ You know that Dan can't actually get rid of homework, but a voter can dream, can't they? It's wishful-thinking voting.

VOTE 4 HALLIE 4 A HALLIELICIOUS SCHOOL!
HOORAY 4 HALLIE-DAYS!

↑ It means nothing, but it's certainly catchy, kind of like political popcorn — it's tasty, but it doesn't fill you up.

There was a meeting after school today for all the candidates. Ms. Oates, my art teacher, led it because she's the Student Council monitor, the one teacher who goes to all the Student Council meetings.

I call her Ms. Oates, even though she wants us to call her "Star." I've tried, but I just can't do it. ↓

She's not the kind of person you would think would do this kind of thing. Being in charge of rules isn't the way she teaches — she encourages freedom and creative expression, that kind of stuff. →

I'm happy to see so many of you running for office. It's an important contribution you're making to our school.

Even if you personally don't win, the students do because you've given them a CHOICE, and CHOICE is what makes democracy work — choosing one set of ideas over another. That's what makes our country strong.

After congratulating us for running, she laid out the rules. Posters can only be a certain size. You can't put your poster over someone else's (and you can't take down your opponents' posters either). Then when the election is over, we're each responsible for cleaning up our own posters.

You're not supposed to "buy" votes, but giving out stuff is okay so long as you give it to EVERYBODY who asks, even people who say they're not voting for you. Handing out fliers is allowed, but littering them all over the place isn't.

There will be a debate where the candidates for president will each give a short statement and then answer students' questions.
The rules are simple.

① No yelling.

② No name-calling.

③ No obscenities.

④ No speaking out of turn or interrupting.

If you break any ONE of those rules, Ms. Oates warned us, you'll be kicked out of the election. Then she made everyone shake hands with everyone else.

I shook the hands of the other kids running for secretary. There are only two of them — like I said, it's not exactly a glamorous position.

Eunice is running for secretary with Eric — they're a team.

Vote double E's! Eunice and Eric!

This is very important work! It must be done neatly.

And it must be done well.

My slogan is "A good night's rest makes school best."

Bettina is running as an independent because she says she's a natural for the job.

That's me — tidy and careful ALL THE TIME!

No boys are running for secretary, which makes me especially suspicious of the job. Maybe it _is_ really like Chief Cafeteria Cook or Head Locker Room Janitor — a title no one wants (unless their friends pressure them to take it, like Carly did with me). I'm sure not neat and thorough, so maybe it would be best if Bettina won — better for her _and_ better for me.

Carly says I'm wrong. She thinks it'll be fun to be on the Student Council together. She thinks we can make real changes and improve our school. I'm just worried about improving my handwriting.

At least secretary is better than being Locker Room Janitor and having to dispose of rotting, smelly socks!

Running for treasurer is different. Either you think it's a really fun job because it involves money (and EVERYONE loves money!) or you want to be on the Student Council, and it's the easiest position you can think of. Or you're like Leah — a superorganized person who knows she's perfect for that kind of work.

Leah

Let's see... there's the money from the bake sale...

...plus the money from the car wash...

...minus expenses for the dance...

...this is just how I budget my allowance.

You can guess why Clayton wants to be treasurer.

Money, money, money, money!

I LOVE money!

That's why I'd make a great treasurer. I LOVE the way that sounds — TREASURE-er!

Jenisse is a cheerleader — that's the experience she brings to the job.

Go, Council, go! Rah, rah, rah! Go, team!

If I can't do it, noone can! Make me TREASURER!

Howard makes it clear why he doesn't want to be president or secretary, but I'm still not sure about treasurer.

I want to be on the Student Council.

But I don't want to give any speeches.

And I'm terrible at taking notes, so vote for me for treasurer!

If the student got their name and the date correct, the rest doesn't really matter.
Chief Test Administrator
Now, that's how a cafeteria should smell—like chocolate chip cookies!
Head Dessert Maker
Adding the pedicure place was a stroke of genius! If kids have beautiful toenails, they'll do beautiful work!
Director of Student Services
Let's get rid of the Presidential Fitness Test and have everyone play on the trampoline instead!
Athletic Director

After the meeting Carly and Leah came over to my house so we could talk about our campaign strategy.

The thing to focus on now is the debate. I've got to be prepared — I have to sound like a strong, smart leader, someone with ideas.

↑
I don't know why Carly's worried. She always sounds smart and strong.

I don't think the debate is a problem. You're a way better speaker than anyone else. The problem is, Hudson's so popular AND he's giving away candy. Those are reasons enough to vote for him.

↑
I agree with Leah. Hudson is tough competition, especially if the election turns into a popularity contest, like most student elections do.

Leah's right. What can we give out that's better than candy but doesn't cost a lot? And it has to be something that reminds kids of Carly.

Even pooling all our allowances, we don't have a big campaign budget. Leah said we should look at what we are rich in — creativity, talent, and artistic skill (since both Leah and me are good at drawing). Those sound like good assets, but how do they translate into an attention-getting giveaway?

We needed a break, so we went into the kitchen for a snack. Unfortunately Cleo was there, chomping on one of her strange sandwich creations. (The worst one was peanut butter, pickle, and avocado – GROSS!) The sight of her made me lose my appetite.

she wasn't exactly cheering everyone else up either.

Hey, Carly, I see you're running against Hudson. He's tough to beat. The only thing kids love more than candy is TV, and you're Miss Anti-TV.

"I'm not anti-TV," Carly said. "I'm against the school force-feeding us ads. I want the TV to be OUR TV."

"That's it!" I yelled. "That's our slogan AND our give-away!"

Everyone looked at me like I was making no sense.

"Here, I'll show you," I explained. I ran back to my room and made a quick model.

It was a small card shaped like a TV set.

CHANGE THE CHANNEL
TAKE OVER COMMERCIAL TV!

You pulled away the card inserted into the TV to see the picture under it.

TAKE OVER COMMERCIAL

CHANGE THE CHANNEL
STUDENT TV!
VOTE 4 CARLY!

The picture beneath showed the school mascot, Rocky Raccoon, and the rest of the slogan.

"See!" I said, demonstrating how the cards worked. "It's a positive message — not anti-TV, but PRO student TV. And it's an active thing. You change the channel by changing the picture."

Even Cleo was impressed. "Not bad," she nodded. "But it'll be a _lot_ of work to make enough of these to hand out to everybody."

She's right! Better get started NOW!

I'll work on my statement for the debate while you make the cards.

Forget about the debate! That's a long way off. You have to help us with this. It's WAY too much work for just two people.

We'll draw and you can cut. We've got to be efficient about this.

Even with the three of us, it was slow going — and BOOOOOOOORING!

The only way to keep ourselves from falling asleep was to spice things up with several different versions of the card.

one with Carly

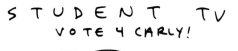

one with lots of kids

one with aliens

Then we started getting really silly. In order to make so many cards, we had to make it fun for ourselves.

In a few days we had finally made enough of the TV cards that we could start giving them out. They turned out to be so cute, everybody wanted one — even the teachers.

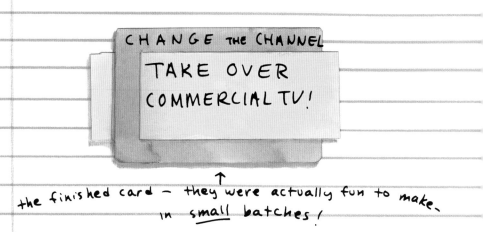

the finished card — they were actually fun to make. in <u>small</u> batches!

Even Hudson liked them. He came up to us at lunch and asked for one.

"Where are those clever cards everyone's talking about?" He winked at Carly. "Don't I get one?"

"Sure," she said, handing him one. "<u>You</u> can vote for me too, you know."

He played with the card and smiled. "Who knows? Maybe I will." He winked again and left.

"Can you believe that?" Leah was outraged. "He's FLIRTING with you! Does he think you'll fall in love with him and drop out of the race? The nerve of him!"

"Look!" I said. "Everyone else seems to be in love with him." A group of girls surrounded him, twittering and giggling. "If he wins, that's why."

Carly shrugged. "He can't help it if girls like him, and there's nothing I can do about it either. I've just got to be as strong a candidate as I can. He can flirt all he wants — he can even ask me out. I'm still running for president."

Leah looked stunned. "You'd go out with him?"

Carly smiled. "Maybe. He is cute. But so what? That doesn't change the election."

Leah didn't say anything after that, but she didn't look happy. I didn't know what to think, so I just finished my lunch, trying not to hear the girls oohing and aahing over something Hudson said. Carly's too smart to turn into one of them, I told myself.

Suddenly I was glad Carly had asked me to run for secretary. What if she'd asked Hudson? Or some other boy?

I wanted to be on her team and help her win. I didn't care about being on the student council — I cared about being Carly's best friend.

As the election gets closer, the campaign posters seem to be multiplying – THEY'RE EVERYWHERE! It's hard to find a space that's not taken. I'm trying to be creative, not only in what the posters say, but in where I put them.

on the basketball backboard ↓

SCORE A POINT FOR CARLY–
VOTE SMART!

above the only drinking fountain that works in the 300 wing ↓

FOR A REFRESHING CHANGE –
CHANGE THE CHANNEL
CARLY 4 PRESIDENT!

MAKE A CHANGE THAT MATTERS!
CHANGE THE CHANNEL
WITH CARLY FOR
PRESIDENT!

↑ by the recycling bins in the cafeteria

GET THE NEWS THAT MATTERS 2 U!
CARLY 4 PREZ!

↑ near the library door

MEDIA CENTER

**E E** VOTE DOUBLE E'S! ERIC AND EUNICE

Bettina a good bet 4 secretary

HUDSON WE LUV U, HUDSON!

$ **J**enisse will make your $$$ COUNT! $

Carly says I'm doing a great job. She hasn't said anything more about Hudson, but I noticed that when he offered her a candy bar, she didn't take it. That's a good sign — she's still more interested in the election than in him. It'd better stay that way!

There's still work to do to get ready for the debate. Leah and I don't have to make a speech, but we're helping Carly with hers, and we've set up a practice debate after school with Leah being Hudson.

**O**livia 4 PREZ! THE PIZZA WINS!

VOTE 4 HOWARD! Y NOT?

He's a star! HUDSON! 4 PRESIDENT !!!

FOR A GOOD NITE'S SLEEP

ERIC 4 PRESIDENT!

VOTE 4 MEL

$ LEAH FOR $ TREASURER

And we're still handing out the TV cards. Hudson keeps sending his friends over to take them, but I know what he's doing — he's making us waste our precious resources on his loyal henchman, people who will never vote for Carly. And there's nothing I can do about it. The campaign rules say giveaways must be for everyone. Otherwise, it's buying votes.

I just clench my teeth and try to get it over with as quickly as possible.

Here! Take it and go away!

That gave me the idea to do the same thing back to them. Now my backpack is FULL of candy bars. I got one by the gym, another in the library, another from some Hudsonite by my locker. Everywhere I go, there's another "Vote for Hudson" campaign worker. How did he get so many people to work for him? Wait a minute, it's obvious — he's PAYING them with candy (something he seems to have an infinite supply of, thanks to his dad).

I asked Ms. Oates if that was allowed. It seemed like buying votes to me.

I know it <u>looks</u> like buying votes to you...

... but it isn't. It's buying workers, and there's nothing in the rules against <u>that</u>.

"Well, there should be!" I was disgusted.

Ms. Oates pursed her lips (something I'd <u>never</u> seen her do before – she's not the pursing lips type).

"We have to work with the rules that are already in place," she said. "If you want to change them for the <u>next</u> election, you'll have to be elected to the Student Council in <u>this</u> one."

I was so exasperated, I wanted to scream. Now I know why kids call her "Astronaut Oates" (instead of "Star" like she wants). She's too far out in space to see how unfair it all is. I guess I should pay more attention to teachers' nicknames. They aren't just arbitrary – there's <u>some</u> truth in them, maybe a <u>lot</u>.

Mr. Lambaste was my mean English and Social Studies teacher last year. Now I have him for Study Hall, which isn't as bad. He's called Mr. L. or Smelly-L or Smell-O because no one likes him – that's reason enough.

Mrs. Church, my math teacher last year, is called "Big Bird." That comes from being called "Mrs. Chirp" first because she's always so cheery. Also she's tall and lanky and when she's excited about some brilliant math equation, she flaps her arms like wings.

Oooh, now wait till we try this with fractions!

Ms. Reilly, my old science teacher, has the nickname "The Professor" because she never stops lecturing. She's a good teacher, but she's always trying to cram more information into you than your brain can hold.

This little factoid about spores and ferns is simply fascinating...

Mr. Hamlin, the other 6th-grade science teacher, is called "Homework Hamlin" because he assigns massive amounts of homework.

I've never seen a worksheet I didn't like. This one is due tomorrow.

Mr. Castillo, the French teacher (the other one, not the one I have), is called "Mr. Caster Oily" because being in his class is like swallowing some nasty medicine.

I hear talking in English! Jamais! En français!!

Ms. Singh has the nickname "Elvis" because she loves Elvis Presley and plays his songs whenever she gets a chance. Sometimes she even sings along. Leah has her for math and thinks she's the best.

I aint nuthin' but a hounddawg!

Mr. Klein, the P.E. teacher, is called "The Devil." No explanation is necessary.

All this candy in school is a DISGRACE. You fatties need to run that sugar off. Everyone take 10 laps— NOW!

Then we'll get serious about calisthenics - and I mean SERIOUS!

I thought maybe I could give Hudson a nickname that would show people who he really is, so they don't just judge him on looks or coolness. But the only nickname that would stick is "Hunk" and I DON'T want him called that. "Weasel" is more like it, but I'm probably the only person who'd use it — except for Leah. She REALLY doesn't trust him.

I heard that Hudson is going to ask Carly to the dance next week. That is so GROSS!

So what if he asks her? She won't say yes.

How do you know?

?

Actually, I didn't know. I hoped, I wanted her to say no. Maybe I could convince her to turn him down. If she was going to say yes in the first place, which I didn't think she'd do.

On the way home from school, I decided to ask Carly about it directly. I was going to say something smooth and persuasive, but I ended up blurting out, "You wouldn't go to the dance with Hudson, would you?"

Carly looked at me, surprised. "Why would he ask me? Isn't he Luanne's boyfriend?"

"They broke up," I said, "and rumor has it he's going to ask you."

Carly smiled. "Well, maybe I _would_ go with him."

"You can't!" I yelled.

She shrugged. "Just because we're competing for the same thing doesn't mean we can't be friends."

"But he's only trying to trick you, to get you to trust him, and then..."

"Then what?" Carly pressed.

I wasn't sure what, but something bad, I knew that. I shook my head. "He's up to something, I'm sure of it." I didn't want to fight with Carly, but the conversation wasn't going at all the way I'd hoped.

Carly stopped walking and cocked her head. "Did you hear that?" she asked.

"Hear what?" Suddenly I was afraid Hudson was spying on us. "I don't hear anything."

"That whimpering noise. It's coming from over there." Carly pointed to some trash.

smelly, rotting vegetables ↓

a good place for a spying rat to hide ⟶

I walked over to the garbage, sure I'd find some kind of rat — human or animal. But it wasn't anything like that.

It was a puppy, a cute, adorable puppy with big, brown eyes. →

It was whimpering and shivering, poor thing. ↙

"Oh, poor baby!" Carly soothed, picking it up. "Look at you — no collar, no owner. Are you lost? Who would leave such a cutie by the trash?"

The puppy wagged its tail and licked Carly's nose for an answer. ↓

"I wish I could take her home," I said (I could see it was a girl). "But my mom has a strict no-pets rule— not even goldfish."

"Maybe I can keep her," Carly said. "I've been begging my parents for a dog forever. They always say no because of my dad's allergies, but I bet if they saw this cutie-pie, they couldn't turn her away. I mean, who could?"

I took the puppy from her, stroking its soft fuzz. I didn't even mind her nipping at my hands — the teeth were so tiny, they were like little pin pricks. I hugged her, and she licked my ear. It tickled so much, I couldn't help laughing.

"You're right. Who could resist such a little furball?" I sighed, and handed her back to Carly. "Only one person — my mom."

"Yeah," Carly agreed. "Your mom is the most unsentimental person I've ever met. I mean, not even a goldfish — that's cold."

I shrugged. "She doesn't like messes."

Carly rolled her eyes. "Like fish are so messy? Yeah, they're always tracking in dirt and clawing at the furniture."

tough choice—
puppy or
fish?
who would
← pick a fish? →

We were planning on going to my house, but now that we had the puppy, we decided to go to Carly's. On the way there we thought of all the reasons we could give for why Carly should get to keep the dog.

By the time we got there, we had a pretty good list.

**Yes, Puppy!**

The puppy needed a good home.

Carly would learn to be SUPER-responsible, since she would do ALL the work.

Carly would vacuum every day to control any dog hair so her dad wouldn't have allergies and her mom would have a clean house.

**No, Puppy**

Carly's dad is allergic.

← All these reasons way outbalance the one lame reason not to keep the dog. Plus Carly's brothers would love the puppy. they've been begging for years to get one. It was a solid case!

At least we thought it was a good list, a clear slam dunk for the puppy. Unfortunately Carly's mom didn't like our list as much as we did.

Now, baby, I know you want a dog and this one is sure cute, no doubt about that!

But you have no idea how much work a dog can be. You have to feed it, walk it, train it, take care of it when it gets sick, clean up its messes.

You have _no_ idea! But the reason I'm saying no isn't about all that. You know why I have to say no and why you shouldn't have even asked in the first place.

I do NOT know that! And how could I NOT ask? Look at this poor thing! She needs a home and you're turning her away coldheartedly. It's not like I went out and got a puppy — this puppy found me!

Ms. Tremain looked sad, but that didn't mean she was going to change her mind.

"Listen, Carly, I know you've already fallen in love with this dog." She reached over and stroked the puppy's head. "But your dad's health comes first. No dogs, not even superadorable ones like this cutie."

"But..." Carly tried again.

"No buts," her mom said firmly. "This isn't about whether you're responsible enough. I _know_ how responsible you are — and believe me, if your dad weren't allergic, I'd say yes in a heartbeat. But he is, and I've seen him when he gets too close to dogs." She shuddered and frowned. "It's _not_ a pretty sight — rashes, swelling, sneezing. Uh, uh!"

"Then what about this poor, innocent puppy?" Carly wailed. "Amelia can't take her - you know her mom!"

And then Ms. Tremain said the dreaded words: "There's alway the animal shelter."

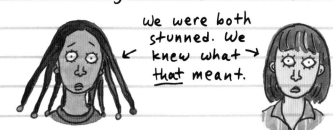

we were both stunned. We ← knew what → that meant.

"Now, don't look at me like that," Ms. Tremain went on. "The animal shelter will find a good home for this baby. That's what they _do_. That's where people go when they're looking to adopt a puppy."

"But," Carly gulped, "if no one picks her, they'll put her to sleep. Isn't that also what they do?"

"Only as a very last resort. It doesn't happen often, and I'm _sure_ someone will give this dog a home." Carly's mom tried to reassure us. I wanted to believe her, but what if it was a bad season for puppies, like there were too many of them or people were too busy to get new pets?

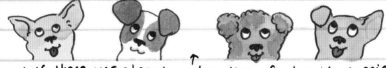

what if there was already a long line of adorable puppies waiting for a home? How could we be sure our puppy would be picked?

Carly and I looked at each other. We were both thinking the same thing. It wasn't good.

The puppy didn't know what to think.

Carly's mom sighed and shook her head. "Look at you two! You'd think I was condemning that poor puppy to death!" She sighed again, loudly. "Oh, all right," she said. "Here's the deal — I'm so sure that somebody will give this baby a home that if she's not adopted by the end of 3 weeks, we'll take her <u>until</u> — and I emphasize ONLY UNTIL — we can find a family for her ourselves. How's that?"

Carly grinned and ran to hug her mom. "Thanks, Mama, I knew you couldn't be cruel to an innocent, sweet puppy."

"Yeah, thanks, Ms. Tremain," I echoed. "We can find someone to take the puppy if we just have some time."

For now, though, we had to keep our part of the deal and take the puppy to the animal shelter. It wasn't far, so Carly and I decided to walk. We tied a rope around the puppy's neck. It felt like she was really ours, at least until we got to the animal shelter.

The puppy wasn't used to a leash and she was so excited, she zigzagged all over the place. When we got tired of untangling the rope, we picked her up and carried her. ↓

We were almost there when we saw Hudson across the street. I would've kept on walking, but he yelled, "Hey!" at Carly (not at me) and smiled. So she stopped and waited for him to catch up to us.

"Hey, yourself," she said. I didn't say anything.

"Cute girl with cute puppy. Where are you going?" He wasn't looking at the dog – he was looking at Carly. Then he leaned down and stroked the puppy's soft head.

"Bite him!" I sent her a mental message. "Bite him HARD!" But my mental telepathy is a bit weak, and the puppy just wagged her whole body and licked Hudson's fingers.

I couldn't believe it — Carly started telling Hudson the whole story, like he was a friend.

...so we're taking her to the shelter and if no one adopts her, we'll come back and keep her until we can find her a home.

I might be able to save you the trouble. I'd love to take her! My parents already said I could have a dog – they're just waiting for some breeder to call. I'll tell them I want this dog.

"Really?" Carly asked. "You'll give her a home?"

"Don't be so surprised!" Hudson laughed. "Who could resist her?" He picked up the puppy and let her lick his ear. "I think I'll name her Munchkin."

I wanted to gag. I mean, I was glad he was taking the puppy. Even if he was a creep, he was better than the animal shelter. But he was so oily-fake, he made my skin crawl. Couldn't Carly see it?

I guess she couldn't because she handed him the rope leash and said, "Thanks, Hudson. You're pretty great."

"I'm the one who should thank you." He smiled that sugary grin again. "Thanks for the puppy - and for the cool story about how you rescued her."

I should have known there was something suspicious about him saying that, but I just wanted to get away.

"We have to get going," I interrupted. "Bye."

"Bye, Carly." Hudson scooped up the puppy and walked off. He looked so pleased with himself, you'd think he'd gotten away with something.

"Come on, Amelia," Carly said. "You just can't believe anything good about Hudson. Stop being so suspicious."

"That's not true!" I disagreed. "It was nice of him to take the puppy — really, that's great. Maybe he'll be a good master, but there's something about him I don't trust."

"That's only because he's my main competition."

Maybe that was it. I hoped for Munchkin's sake he was a nice person.

HE KNOWS HIS STUFF!
UNDERSTANDS STUDENTS!
DOES HIS BEST!
SUPER GUY!
ON TOP OF THINGS!
NAME HIM PRESIDENT!!

V
O
T
E

CHANGE THE CHANNEL
CARLY!
VOTE FOR STUDENT CONTROL OVER TV!

You see these posters ALL OVER school.

We have to squeeze in Carly's posters →

We needed to forget about Hudson the person and Hudson the puppy rescuer. It was time to focus on Hudson the candidate.

The debate is coming up, and Carly needs to do way better than Hudson in it. I know she's been practicing a lot. Leah and I have heard her statement so many times, we could almost give it for her.

This isn't another boring speech about being "on the threshold of a new millenium."

This is a speech about us— about what we can do to actively guide our own education.

Carly's a pro. No matter how much she likes Hudson (and she's still not admitting anything), she's not going to go easy on him in the debate. She's an expert arguer, no matter how sugary or sleazy Hudson might get.

So I'm not worrying about that. I have something else on my mind. Our campaign posters keep disappearing. Every time I put up a new "Vote to Change the Channel! Vote for Carly" banner, by the next day it's gone. You would think someone would have seen who's taking down the posters, but no one knows — or no one's telling. Naturally, I have my suspicions.

# POSSIBLE POSTER PILFERERS

The first choice would be someone campaigning for the same office. That means all the other presidential candidates.

Hudson — why would he bother? He's so popular, does he need to cheat? He shouldn't, but he's the one I trust the least.

Olivia — she doesn't seem mean enough. Besides, I get the feeling she doesn't care enough about winning to bother.

Eric — I guess it could be him, but I actually like Eric, so I hope not. He has a good sense of humor and isn't the sleazy type.

Cassandra — she definitely cares a LOT about winning, but if it's her, why doesn't she take down other posters, not just Carly's?

Sandro — I still haven't figured out why he's even running. His slogan is "Make my day - vote for Sandro." I want to know why I should care?

Hallie — she thinks it's a beauty contest, not a political election. And the way some guys look at her, she may be right.

Or the poster thief could be an enemy of Carly, someone who doesn't like her. That's a pretty short list.

Maxine — she's been mad at Carly ever since she dumped her as a friend— I mean, Maxine dumped Carly, not the other way around. She thought Carly would be devastated and pine away for her. And maybe Carly would have, but she figured out what a manipulative creep Maxine is and let her know it!

Graham — he's been nasty to Carly because he asked her to a dance and she said no. She didn't mean to hurt his feelings and she turned him down as nicely as she could, but he still hasn't forgiven her. Now he says she's a stuck-up snob and he wouldn't go out with her if she begged him. Really?

After Hudson, who's suspect #1, I think it's probably someone from the second group, even though there are fewer suspects. Maxine seems the most likely to me. Leah is sure it's Hudson. Carly says she has no idea and doesn't really care (except she's sure it's NOT Hudson).

She thinks we should focus on putting up new posters and not worry about what happened to the old ones. That's easy for her to say — it's a lot of work to make new posters and find some space to put them. And then the next day I have to do the same thing all over again. The posters are getting pretty sloppy.

The first batch looked good.
↓

**CHANGE THE CHANNEL!**
VOTE FOR
**C**ARLY
TV BY THE STUDENTS, FOR THE STUDENTS, AND OF THE STUDENTS.

The second batch was okay.
↓

VOTE 4 CHANGE
VOTE 4 STUDENT POWER
VOTE 4 CARLY 4 PREZ!

The third batch looked kind of desperate.
↓

I SAID:
VOTE 4 CARLY!
DO IT!

I thought I might get an idea of who was taking down the posters if some other candidate's always took their place, but that's no indication. Once a new poster for Eric went up where one of Carly's was. Another time, it was a poster for Jenisse, who's not even running for president — she wants to be treasurer. Sometimes the space is even left blank. There's no suspicious pattern to it.

I tried to trick Maxine into admitting that she was the culprit.

She acted like she didn't understand what I was saying. Maybe I should have been more direct.

Leah tried a different tactic. She followed Hudson around all day, but she didn't have any more success than I did.

Carly said it's time to stop worrying about the posters. We have a debate to win — tomorrow!

The key to public speaking is to talk loudly, clearly, and slowly.

And to be passionate about your point of view— no dull monotone, no boring mumbling, no droning on and on.

I'm glad it's not me going up there in front of the whole school. Carly will do a great job. She's not nervous at all.

# How to Give a Great Speech

Ten Easy Tips to Terrific Public Speaking

I did it my waaaaaaaay!

1. Pretend you aren't giving a speech, but doing spoken karaoke— ham it up and have fun!

6. Use audiovisual props — that way you'll have your audience's attention even if you don't speak well.

7. Turn your speech into a jump-rope rhyme. You'll be so busy jumping, you'll forget to be nervous.

8. Make your speech short and exciting — that way no one will get bored and you'll have less time to make a mistake.

9. Use a phone as a prop. Don't actually make a call — just holding it to your ear while you talk will make you much more relaxed.

10. Forget about the speech and just offer to answer questions instead.

THE GREAT

Carly doesn't need any of those tips. She's a natural speaker. ↓

Eric was in his pajamas and bathrobe just like I suggested in tip #6. ↙

↑ I was more nervous watching her than she was standing in front of the whole school! She was great, like I knew she would be, and kids clapped the loudest for her.

↑ Eric was okay, except he tried to make his point about how tired starting school at 8:00 am. makes him by falling asleep in the middle of his speech!

↑ Hallie chose the short and sweet method – "Hello." (BIG smile.) "Vote for me. Bye!"

↑ Sandro turned his speech into a cheerleading cheer. It woke everyone up after Eric and Hallie.

# DEBATE

Ms. Oates was the moderator, of course.

↑ she introduced everyone, made sure no one talked too long (NOT a problem), then asked questions for the debate part.

↑ Cassandra was <u>so</u> technical, it was hard to focus on what she was saying — "wireless Internet... speed of transmission... amount of data..." It was more of a lecture than a speech.

↑ I have to admit Hudson was okay. He didn't say anything fascinating, but he was loud, clear, and concise. He talked more about candy than student government, and some kids thought that was a GOOD thing.

↑ Olivia started by reading a recipe for pizza. It sounds like a catchy idea, but if you've ever read a recipe out loud, you know how boring that can be. It's like reading the phone book!

Ms. Oates asked questions like "Why should you represent all the other students to the school administration? What can you do for them that no one else can?" I wouldn't have known what to say — and some of the candidates had that same problem. Olivia, for example, said, "I would speak out for pizza lovers everywhere!" Sounds okay, but what does it **mean**? Eric said he would sleep through Student Council meetings, so the principal would get the hint that school starts too early. And that's supposed to make us want to vote for him?

Hudson acted like he was giving students exactly what they wanted when he promised that he — and only he — could deliver a candy-snack machine to every hallway. I wonder if that's **really** what kids want and need. I'm all for the occasional snack, but in **every** hallway? We'll have the fattest school ever!

← But Hudson made a convincing sales pitch. He had something to offer that nobody else could give.

The way everyone applauded, you would think he was promising each kid their own home-theater system, not a fast-track to no more money and a lot more tummy.

typical student before the installation of all the candy machines ↓

after ↓

I'm hungry!

I'm thirsty!

where can I spend my allowance?

I'm broke.

And so is the chair I sat in.

I wish he'd brought some visual aids — a graphic before-and-after picture would have been better than any argument he could make.

Carly, of course, answered all the questions better than anyone. She was smart and funny and had great ideas. She was SO much better than the others, the election seemed like a slam dunk — even if we lost all of our posters.

I ran to hug her afterward. →

*Congratulations, you were GREAT!*

*Thanks! It was actually fun.*

A whole mob of kids came up to say how well Carly did and that they would definitely vote for her. She made a BIG impression. But Hudson had a circle of kids around him, too — not as many as Carly (that made me smile), but more than anyone else except her.

"I think you've got Hudson beat," I said.

Carly grinned. "And you were worried I'd go easy on him — as if I'd lose on purpose! I want to win, no matter how cute my main opponent is."

Leah clapped Carly on the back. "You want to win this thing because you want to make a difference. The other kids are running for office to have fun or to test how popular they are. You're the only one with a serious plan."

"I don't know about that," Carly said. "Hudson's serious about his plan too."

"Candy machines everywhere? That's a plan?"
Leah frowned. "That's just about making money —
for his dad. He's the one with the vending machine
company. I bet Hudson gets a cut."

"Yeah," I agreed. "Who really benefits from
the machines? Hudson's dad will make a fortune!"
It all seemed sleazy to me.

Just then Maya walked up,
munching on a candy bar.

"Carly, you were terrific!" she said.
"I'm voting for you, but after you win,
could you work with Hudson to get
at least a couple of those candy
machines? Have you tried the Mellow
Bars? They're delicious!"

"If I win, getting vending machines isn't high on my
list of priorities. I have to be honest with you — if
you really want candy, you should vote for Hudson."

Maya looked hurt. "I think you'd be a better
president."

Carly sighed. "I guess I'm worried a lot of kids
will think that but will still vote for Hudson because
they like chocolate. I can't keep his promises."

"If they do that, then they're stupid voters and they'll get what they deserve," I said.

"Yeah? What about the rest of us?" Leah demanded. "I don't even like candy! So you're saying I'll be stuck with Hudson because other kids can't control their appetites?"

"I'm not saying anything like that." Carly took the candy wrapper from Maya, wadded it up, and pitched it into the trash can. "I'm just saying I hope people will vote for who will make the best president, not who will fill their stomach with sugar. And if you vote for me," she looked at Maya, "it should be because you support me, not because you want me to follow some other guy's plan, especially when it's one I don't agree with."

"You're right, Carly, I'm sorry." Maya did look sorry. "I just have a soft spot for Mellow Bars."

Carly and I looked at each other. We were both worried that a lot of kids were like Maya. That meant no matter how great Carly was in her speech or the debate, she wouldn't win. Kids would choose chocolate over anything else.

Carly might have been worried about Hudson getting votes for candy, but Hudson was worried too. He knew that Carly had done better in the debate than he had. He hadn't seemed smart or capable or funny — Eric came off better than him in those areas. Hudson acted like a candy salesman, not a president.

I could tell he was worried because he started giving out lots more chocolate — so much candy that the principal decided the giveaways were getting out of control and he banned any more handouts.

That made Hudson even more nervous. Without the temptation of sugar, how would he get enough votes? At lunch I heard him arguing with his friends, yelling that they weren't any help now that they weren't giving out chocolate. And he isn't flirting with Carly anymore either. He doesn't even look at her when he passes by.

Candy wrappers were everywhere, and kids were manic on sugar highs. The teachers hated it!

Carly doesn't look at him either. She acts like she doesn't care, but I can tell she does.

And you thought Hudson was going to ask me to the dance! As if!

It's only a week until the election, and Hudson must be feeling desperate because he did something really ugly, something I never would have thought him capable of, even at his sleaziest.

He started a smear campaign against Carly. And he used the puppy to do it.

Leah was the first to notice something was wrong. "What's going on, Carly?" she asked. "People are looking at you funny. There's some kind of rumor spreading about you — and it's NOT a good one. Do you know what kids are saying?"

She didn't. I didn't. We hadn't heard a thing. As we walked to the library, Carly turned to notice every kid we passed. When she smiled and waved at people she knew, <u>no one</u> smiled back. They wouldn't look her in the face.

"You're right!" Carly wailed. "It's something really horrible — no one will even glance at me. What is it?"

"Come on, think!" I said. "Did ANYTHING happen that could have made someone mad at you? Did you have a fight with anyone? Is Maxine up to her old tricks, writing nasty notes about you instead of to you?"

Carly shook her head. She looked really upset, like she would cry any minute.

As soon as we came into the library, everyone turned to stare at us — and not in a good way — then they started whispering to each other. It felt like we'd walked in without any clothes on.

It was like one of those nightmares where you're at school and you realize you forgot to get dressed — only this wasn't a bad dream, it was real!
↓

First I felt terrible, but then I got mad. We hadn't done ANYTHING to deserve that kind of treatment, and I was going to find out what was behind it all.

I marched up to the closest knot of kids.

"Hey!" I hissed. "What's going on? Why is everyone looking at us like that?"

"It's not you," a girl answered. "It's Carly. She seemed so cool, but to practically murder a puppy..."

"What _are_ you talking about?" I squawked.

"You don't know?" Her eyebrows shot up and almost flew off her forehead. She was excited to find someone who didn't know such juicy gossip and she couldn't wait to tell me.

It was ugly — very ugly. And it was Hudson who started it all.

He needed a weapon to use against Carly, and he chose the cutest, softest, sweetest thing he could find. →

MUNCHKIN! ←

According to this girl, Hudson had the puppy with him after school yesterday. Naturally puppies are people magnets and everyone came up to pet her and ooh over how adorable she was. (He'd tied a bandanna around her neck, so she was especially cute.)

Then, as kids played with Munchkin, he told them how he found her when Carly was taking her to the animal shelter. Hudson claimed Carly was going to abandon Munchkin to an awful fate when he stepped in and rescued her. He insisted he would give the puppy a good home since Carly was so cruelly throwing her away.

"He saved that puppy's life," the girl finished. "I had no idea Carly was that cold."

"She's not!" I snapped. "The whole thing is a lie from start to finish. I was there — I know!"

Suddenly everyone was staring at me, waiting for my explanation. →

I was ready to scream at all of them that Hudson was a manipulative creep! ↙

Except I had the sinking feeling that no one would believe me. After all, we _were_ taking Munchkin to the shelter, and Hudson _did_ adopt her and give her a home. The other details — that Carly would have come back for the puppy if no one took her — sounded suspiciously like a lame lie.

"Well?" the girl asked. "What really happened?"

"Hudson twisted the facts — Carly was never going to abandon the puppy." I knew I sounded desperate even as I said it.

"Uh-huh," the girl nodded, looking like she didn't believe a word. "Right. Sure." Her friends smiled and nodded too. "But she _was_ taking the puppy to the animal shelter?" she pressed.

"Yes, but..." I bit my lip. I was afraid I was confirming the ugly rumor rather than refuting it. "Her mom said she had to wait a couple of weeks, but if no one took the puppy home, then Carly could come back and get her."

"So Hudson told the truth?" It was like she didn't even hear my explanation.

I always thought of the → truth as a single thing, whole and simple.

← Now I saw how it could be chopped up, crumbled, turned upside-down and not be the truth at all.

"No!" I yelled. "I mean, yes, kind of, a sliver of the truth, a crumb, but NOT the whole thing." I gave up. I went back to Carly and Leah and explained what had happened.

"He's using Munchkin against you," I summed it up. "And who can resist those big, brown puppy-dog eyes?"

"That makes me sick!" said Leah. "It's like false advertising — he's telling enough of the truth to be trustworthy, but leaving out the most important parts so people will get the wrong impression. It's a total distortion!"

Carly was crushed.

It's like saying, "Eat candy - it will give you energy" without mentioning it will also make you fat.

What do I do now? This is about more than the election — it's about my reputation! I don't want people thinking I'd abandon a puppy!

"We just have to show kids that it's spin, not fact — it's Hudson's false interpretation of what happened, not what really happened," I said.

"But how do we do that?" Carly asked. "Once a rumor is started, it's almost impossible to stop. It takes on a life of its own."

Carly was right. We needed a whole new campaign —
right away! I stayed up late that night and made a
whole new series of posters, not to get Carly elected,
but to clear her name.

I think they turned out pretty good. I just hope
they do the job!

↓

Cigarette companies used
to say that smoking
was GOOD for you.

Now they admit that it's
hazardous to your health.

How do you know what
to believe?

GET THE WHOLE TRUTH!
CARLY IS
INNOCENT!!

If it looks like a
duck and quacks like
a duck, is it always
a duck?

Yes, UNLESS it's a
rubber ducky!

GET THE WHOLE TRUTH!

CARLY IS
INNOCENT!

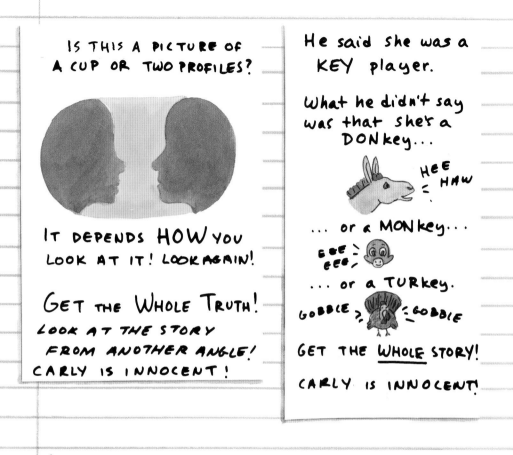

I don't know if it's enough, but it's something. Not everyone avoids Carly now, and some kids are looking at Hudson suspiciously.

Carly was looking differently at Hudson too. She was furious and couldn't wait to confront him.

"He's not the least bit sorry!" Carly was so angry, she was shaking. "And the worst part is, he's getting away with it. Your posters are great and they're helping people figure out the whole truth, but not soon enough. I can't bear the thought that he'll win the election because of such an ugly smear campaign."

"Come on." I put my arm around her. "He hasn't won yet. Tomorrow's the election — we'll see what happens." I tried to sound positive, but I was worried myself.

In Study Hall I could barely focus on what Mr. L. was saying (he always welcomes us with some news tidbit). Then I heard something that caught my attention — something about the election.

Unfortunately recent elections have been more about image than substance, more about sound bites than sound policy. Before you vote tomorrow, ask yourself what you know about each candidate.

Think about how they behaved during the campaign. Don't turn your ballot into a popularity contest.

Normally I think Mr. L. is an awful person, but for today he was my favorite teacher. I hoped everyone would listen to him.

# ELECTION DAY!

I was glad Carly and I had French together last period. That's when the election results were going to be announced. For most kids it was a normal school day except they took the time to vote. For Carly, Leah, and me it was the most jittery day ever. All I could think of was what would happen if we won — and what would happen if we lost. It was like being on a seesaw all day.

"Attention, students," the P.A. crackled. "The results of the Student Council election have now been tallied. For the office of treasurer — Leah Cox."

"Leah!" Carly and I jumped up from our desks and hugged each other. Leah won! And if she had won, that meant...

"...of secretary — Amelia..."

"I WON!" I screamed. I hadn't thought about ME winning, I'd been so focused on Carly. All the kids started clapping. Even Mr. Le Poivre joined in.

I hugged Carly again. "That means you won too!" I said. She grinned. We were both so relieved.

"...office of president..."
We waited for her name, ready to cheer again.
"... Hudson Strauss. Congratulations to the new
Student Council, and thank you to all the candidates."
Hudson?! Not Carly? I couldn't believe it.
I thought for sure that if Leah and I were elected,
Carly was too. Was it some kind of mistake?
Should we ask for a
recount?

The worst part is that creep gets rewarded for lying.

No, I take that back— the worst part is that now he's our president. UGH! It makes me want to change schools.

I didn't know what to think. Now Leah and I
would be on the Student Council WITH HUDSON!
I didn't even want to be on the Student Council,
not without Carly. It wasn't supposed to happen
this way.

What a disaster! We have to work with that slimeball? It'll be torture!

I only ran for secretary to be with you, Carly. Maybe I should quit. Can I quit?

"No way! You can't quit!" Carly argued. "You and Leah have to balance whatever Hudson does. You need to be there now more than ever."

It wasn't what I'd imagined when we started the campaign, but I was stuck with it.

Leah → felt the same way I did — it wasn't right for us to be elected and not Carly.

Carly tried to be a good sport and told us we'd be great.

But it all felt wrong, very wrong.

The next day I bumped into Hudson. I thought he would be gloating, really pleased with himself for winning, but he wasn't. In fact, he almost looked scared.

"What's up?" I asked him. "Now that you're president, you're worried you might actually have to do some work?."

"Huh? No, that's not it." He practically ran away.

I wondered what was wrong, he was acting so odd. I didn't have to wait long to find out. As I sat down in Study Hall, the P.A. system came on.

"It has come to our attention that one of the candidates in yesterday's election broke the rule about respecting opponents' campaign posters. Because he took down Carly Tremain's posters, Hudson Strauss is disqualified."

The office of president goes to the candidate with the next-highest vote total, Carly Tremain."

I was stunned. Hudson was the one taking down our posters! And now Carly was president? I couldn't believe it — the creep didn't get caught for his lie, but for something else! It was enough to give me back my faith in elections.

I didn't realize that Mr. L. was talking until he said something that grabbed my attention — it was about the election again.

...if I hadn't seen young Mr. Strauss IN THE ACT — yes, red-handed in the very act — of removing one of Miss Tremain's posters. It takes vigilance to keep democracy safe, constant vigilance against corruption and abuses of power. Each of you is responsible for protecting democracy!

So it was Mr. L. who caught Hudson! Now he is definitely my favorite teacher, no matter how mean he acts! I'll never call him Smell-O again!

I couldn't wait to see Carly and Leah! Now we'll all be on the Student Council together, just the way we planned. And Hudson got exactly what he deserved — NOTHING! It was hard to say which was more satisfying.

There was a throng of kids around Carly after school, all congratulating her. She looked really happy.

"Great campaign!" Maya said. "I'm so glad you're president. I want to lobby you for something, for one small favor."

"Sure," said Carly. "It's my job to listen. What is it?"

"How about a candy machine, just one — in the cafeteria, not in any hallways? Please! I'm addicted to those Mellow Bars, really!" Maya pleaded.

Carly laughed. "I'll bring it up with my fellow council members, okay? I'm not promising anything more than that."

"Fine, fine," Maya said quickly. "That's great. Maybe you can make a story about it for the student news channel — 'Candy comes to school to add sweetness to classes.' Something like that."

We'd better get busy with the student TV idea. After all, the next election is only a year away.

I could see → it now.

This is Amelia with a late-breaking story about the election. It has drama, comedy, a dash of mystery — who took the posters all wrapped up in a patriotic campaign. But first a word from our sponsor — Mellow Bars!

# Amelia's Quick Back-to-School Guide
## to Surviving School Elections or Oral Reports

① If you decide to run, run with a friend. It's more fun that way.

I'll be president if you'll be vice president.

How about I be president, and you be vice president?

Let's rock-paper-scissors for that.

Great! Democracy in action! Or pure chance!

② Think of as many catchy slogans as you can. Use all the alliteration around!

Hello, Helena, your happy, HAPPY president!

**P**ERFECT
**P**LEASANT
**P**ROUD
**P**ERKY
**P**RESIDENTIAL
THAT'S HELENA!

Those are catchy?

③ Learn how to speak loudly and clearly in public. No mumbling allowed! No ums, ers, or you knows!

I'd rather die than give a talk to a huge crowd of strangers— all staring at me!

Can't someone else give my speech for me? I'll pay!

④ Pretend you're talking to yourself in the bathroom mirror. It's easier that way — you can even sing!

I'm the best, oh yeah!

Yeah, baby! I'm the best!

# GENERAL BACK-TO-SCHOOL-AND-BEYOND SURVIVAL TIPS

① Don't bring too much stuff to school the first day — or any day. Chances are, you won't need it.

② Make sure you brush your teeth, wash your face, and comb your hair. First impressions count!

③ Do NOT bring milk or juice in your lunch and then throw your backpack around. You will regret it for days!

squashed, leaking milk container ↓

soggy, stinky milk-or-juice-stained binders, papers, everything! ↙

④ Do bring a notebook! You never know when you'll get a great idea and need to write it down.

I wish the dog ate my homework!

Can I turn this in?

Just a reminder to myself — don't throw your back-pack around until after lunch.

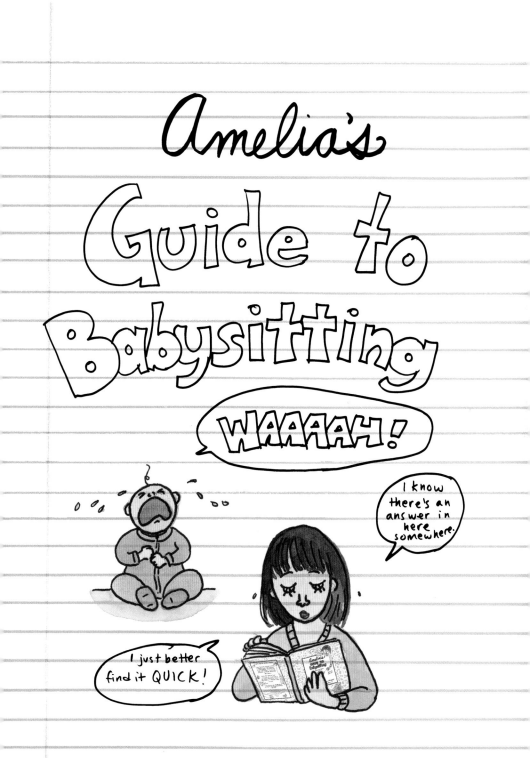

I've tried a lot of ways to make money. Dog walking was a disaster! The dogs ended up walking me instead of the other way around.

Selling lemonade went sour. The only people who ended up drinking it were me and Carly, my best friend and business partner.

So when Carly said she had a great idea for how we could make LOTS of money AND have fun together at the same time, I was all ears.

Now that we're older, we can do jobs we couldn't do before.

Like babysitting! My brothers earn big bucks that way.

Babysitting! Of course! My sister, Cleo, babysits a lot and she always has money, like Carly's brothers do. And I even have some experience (unlike the dog-walking fiasco, where I had no idea what I was getting myself into since I've never owned a dog). I've taken care of my baby half brother a few times. I didn't get paid, but it still counts as experience.

George is my half brother (not half of a brother) because my dad remarried and started a new family. They don't live close by — in fact, they're an airplane ride away in Chicago — but whenever I visit, I end up watching George, which is okay because he's very cute and I love him.

Having experience means I know how much work babysitting is — it's not exactly a walk in the park. I don't mind (too much) with George because he's my half brother (and he's so much nicer than my whole sister). But it's still not easy. When he was really little, I had a hard time guessing what he wanted when he cried. It's better now that he can talk, but it's still exhausting. So I wasn't sure about Carly's idea.

"I dunno," I told her. "Babysitting is work!"

"Jobs usually are. If it wasn't, why would someone pay you?"

She had a point. I admit when I first imagined taking care of George, I thought he would just smile or sleep the whole time. He didn't do either.

Wouldn't it be great to get paid to do nothing — just to be there in case of emergency, which, of course, would never actually happen? After all, it's called babysitting, so it should involve resting and relaxing, not ← running around.

Baby's asleep somewhere over here. →

"Anyway," said Carly, "it's not hard work. Especially if we do it together – then it'll be FUN!"

"But what if I don't like the kid?" I asked. "George can drive me crazy, but he's my brother, so I have to put up with him."

"Don't worry about liking the kid. You can stand anyone for a short time. After all, you live with Cleo and you survived the mean Mr. L. for a teacher last year."

She was right, but those people were bad examples. I didn't have a choice about Cleo or Mr. L. — believe me, if I had, things would be way better! With the kids we babysat, I could always say no. I might want to say no.

"Okay," Carly tried again. "Think of it this way – do you like money?"

I felt sorry for my empty piggy bank. He deserved a meal or two. That was worth dealing with a baby Cleo or Mr. L.

Remember, you said you'd feed me!

"And we'll be working together," Carly added. "That makes anything easier to face."

That convinced me. I can handle tough stuff if I have Carly's help. One thing that made Mr. L.'s meanness so extra mean was that Carly wasn't in that class with me.

"You're right," I said. "Count me in!"

So it's set. We're starting a babysitting business where we always work together. That means only earning half as much money, since we'll split it, but it'll be _twice_ as much fun. Thats the kind of math I like!

DOUBLE BEE'S

2 BABYSITTERS FOR THE PRICE OF 1!

Day or night! Call 831-0602   Night or day!

Carly wants to call us the Double Bee's. She's even designed a flyer to put up on the library bulletin board to drum up business. She was all prepared before she asked me!

I know Carly can handle anything. That's just the kind of person she is. But I'm not so sure if I'll be a great babysitter. Before we start, I want to be prepared too, so I'm making this guide. By the time I'm done, I'll know how to handle finicky eaters and bath times, tantrums and hiccups — everything a babysitter might need!

Carly says she'll help.

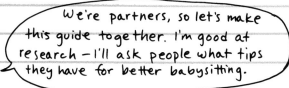

We're partners, so let's make this guide together. I'm good at research — I'll ask people what tips they have for better babysitting.

And I'll make charts, quizzes, and lists. We'll be super-prepared, ready for ANYTHING.

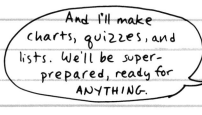

When Cleo saw what we were working on, she laughed. She said those who can, do. Those who can't, make guides and tell <u>other</u> people what to do. She said we don't need a guide, we need experience. Kids are going to run us ragged. That's what <u>she</u> thinks! I told her we'd show her how wrong she is.

Tell you what — you want to prove me wrong, I'll give you a chance to. I'm supposed to babysit for the Reeses this Saturday. I'll tell them I can't but you can.

Our first job already?! Carly and I didn't think twice. We both said, "Great, we'll do it!" But then I wondered, what if Cleo is setting us up? What if the Reese kids are horrible brats?

It was as if Cleo could read my mind.

And don't worry — the Reese kids aren't monsters. They're just normal kids. Ruthy is 5 and Tyler is 7. How hard can it be?

It sounded good, except how come now she was saying how easy it would be when before she said it would be too hard for us? I guess we'd just have to find out. If it was a set-up, at least Carly would be there to help me out — and we'd never trust Cleo again.

So it's all set. In three days we have our first real job!

I wanted to find out <u>before</u> our job what kind of babysitter I would be, so I made a quiz to see if I'm like Cleo, Gigi, Carly, or Leah. If it turns out I'm like Cleo, I should quit now, but if I'm like Carly, I'm ready for anything.

## QUIZ #1

# WHAT KIND OF BABYSITTER ARE YOU?
### (for older kids, not babies)

| ① With little kids, how do you spend most of your time? | | | |
|---|---|---|---|
| ⓐ Showing them how to be clean and tidy. | ⓑ Playing with them. | ⓒ Ignoring them. | ⓓ Yelling at them. |

See how easy it is to fold underwear?

Now STOP picking your nose!

Uh-oh! Another chute— I'm losing!

And I got a ladder—I'm winning!

...then he said that she was imagining it all...

I'm hungry!

Can I please have dinner now? PLEASE!!

And don't come out of your room until I say so!

Wow, the thrill of power!

② As a special treat, you're willing to:
ⓐ let them eat cookies so long as they do it OUTSIDE.
ⓑ do a fun art project.
ⓒ play a game so long as you can watch TV at the same time.
ⓓ let them help with your homework.
I see a CRUMB!
It's all in my mouth, honest!
We're going to make a cool surprise for your parents.
Roll the dice for me, will ya?
Whaddya mean you don't know how to solve for the value of x? Don't they teach you anything in first grade?

③ How do you handle dinner?
ⓐ Quickly and efficiently.
ⓑ Warm and friendly.
ⓒ Casually and easily.
ⓓ Sloppily, but it's not your kitchen, so who cares?
No muss, no fuss.
Do I have to eat wearing a rain poncho?
Let's go around the table telling knock-knock jokes. You go first!
Knock, knock!
Sure, you can eat dinner in front of the TV so long as you watch my show.
At least I concocted an interesting dish!

④ What best describes your attitude toward bath time?
ⓐ Scrub, scrub, scrub!
ⓑ Add lots of bubble bath to make extra fun.
ⓒ A washcloth wipe is good enough.
ⓓ The kids aren't that dirty—why bother?
Not in the ears!
Yes, the ears!
Wheeee!
Clean enough?
Sure, kid!
You really only need a bath when you begin to smell.
Yeah!

⑤ Name one of your favorite things to do while babysitting.
ⓐ Organizing closets.
ⓑ Playing with all the toys you remember from when you were little.
ⓒ Your nails.
ⓓ Watching TV even if it's kiddie cartoons.
It's so satisfying to straighten things up!
Play-Doh—my favorite!
And how about Twister!
And Candyland—yum!
Now, that's a nice color!
As soon as you're in bed, I'm changing the channel!

⑥ What is the best way to deal with a temper tantrum?
ⓐ Tidy up the place.
ⓑ Calmly but firmly.
ⓒ Lock yourself in the bathroom.
ⓓ Panic and call 911.
It's hard to be angry when everything's all neat and clean, so now you can calm down. Well, at least I'm calmer.
You can cry all you want, but nothing can happen until you quiet down.
You mean it's not working?
Nope.
La, la, LA! I can't hear you!
HELP! The kid's about to EXPLODE!

⑦ What is the best way to handle discipline?
ⓐ Avoid kids who need it.
ⓑ Calmly but firmly.
ⓒ With an iron fist.
ⓓ By yelling.
I'm sorry, Mr. Smith, I'm busy that night. And that night too. I'm really busy...
...for the next year.
Both of you need to say you're sorry. Hitting never solved anything.
Yeah, but it feels good.
Not if you're the one who's hit.
That's it—no dessert for you. And no TV, either.
But I didn't do anything!
You were THINKING of doing something!
WHAT DID I SAY?!
I SAID TIME OUT—NOW!

| ⑧ What do you like to read to the kid before bed time? | | | |
|---|---|---|---|
| ⓐ A book that hasn't been drooled or chewed on. | ⓑ As many books as possible - it's fun to do the different voices. | ⓒ The shortest book in the house. | ⓓ Your own book, to yourself. |

Ew! Not this one!

But it's a delicious story.

And the Big Billy Goat Gruff said ...

... the end! Time to sleep!

Huh?

It's my homework, so it's definitely boring. I'm sure you don't want me to read it to you.

| ⑨ How do you put a child to bed? | | | |
|---|---|---|---|
| ⓐ With the least fuss possible. | ⓑ With a story or a lullaby. | ⓒ Pull back covers, insert child, pull up covers. | ⓓ As soon as possible. Right after dinner is the best. |

Your teeth are brushed?

Yep.

All cleaned up?

Yep.

Okay then, good night!

'night.

And then the princess broke the magic spell...

That's that.

Nighty night!

But it's not even dark yet.

It will be when you close your eyes.

If you answered mostly a's, you have a lot of potential as a babysitter, but you need to relax and not worry about messes so much. With little kids, they're hard to avoid. You're a neat freak, like Leah (the kind of person who folds underwear).

If you answered mostly b's, you're a terrific babysitter for any age! You have a lot of patience and genuinely like little kids. You're like Carly.

*I didn't answer all b's, but enough so that I'm here — that's good news!*

If you answered mostly c's, you need to think less about yourself and more about the kid you're taking care of. You could be great at this job if you'd just try to have more fun (the kind a little kid can enjoy). Still, you do the job fine. You're like Gigi.

If you answered mostly d's, you're doing the bare minimum. Why don't you find work that fits better with your personality, something where you won't hurt kids' feelings, something more impersonal, like filing papers or hoeing weeds? You're not nice enough to be a good babysitter. You're like Cleo.

*What do you know? Kids LOVE me!*

I did so well on the quiz, I felt pretty confident about our job. I could tell Carly wasn't worried at all.

Saturday at 1 p.m. we walked over to the Reeses (they live 3 doors down — very convenient). The mom and dad seemed very nice, the house was clean and organized, and the kids seemed really sweet. Plus the parents left us brownies and pizza to eat — I grade them an A+ for that.

Ruthy just wanted us to read books to her.

Tyler wanted help building with Legos.

They were both completely easy to take care of. All we had to do was play with them. They even put away their toys when we asked them to. I didn't have to worry about not liking them or that they wouldn't like me. It was all a piece of cake.

In fact, it was so easy, I thought there was no point to finishing the guide. I mean, there's nothing to babysitting. I was worried for nothing. I couldn't wait to tell Cleo how wrong she was.

And she couldn't wait to hear how it went. As soon as we got home, Cleo was there, asking us questions.

"So," she said. "Not as easy as you thought, eh?"

Carly laughed. "You're right — it wasn't. It was even _easier_! Those kids are great and the parents are the kind you _want_ to babysit for."

Cleo looked surprised. Then she smiled. "Well, if it was like that, you won't mind babysitting them again _next_ Saturday, only this time, it's all day, from 7 a.m. to around midnight. Think you're up for that?"

Carly and I looked at each other. We didn't see trouble — we saw dollar signs! This was WAY better than trying to sell lemonade.

⟵ 17 hours! We'd be RICH! ⟶

"You really don't mind giving us your job?" Carly asked. "That's a lot of money."

"I know," said Cleo, "but I really want to go to a concert with Gigi. You'd be doing me a favor."

Since she put it that way, naturally we said yes.
Now our problem is deciding what to do with all the
money we'll make. I _love_ having that kind of problem.

Now I think I'll keep making the guide anyway. Not
because babysitting is hard, but because there are lots
of things you need to know about when you babysit,
including stuff that has nothing to do with the kids.
Like food. What kind of snacks are available is
more important than it might seem.

## RATE THE SNACKAGE QUOTIENT

**HIGH** — The best, meaning the tastiest snacks
around. Chips, microwave popcorn,
pretzels — salty foods are GOOD! Ice
cream is also good so long as it's a
flavor like Chocolate Fudge, not a
strange grown-up flavor like Maple.

The highest
rating — the
Full Tummy.

**MEDIUM** —
Okay, there are lots of healthy foods
like fruit and carrots, but there's
also cheese and crackers and chocolate-
chip cookies. If there's chocolate, there's hope.

The next-best
rating — the
No-complaints
Tummy.

**LOW** – The worst possible choices, meaning food that has all the flavor sucked out of it, like all-organic, vegan snacks. No bread, cheese, chips, nothing with any taste to it. Quinoa pretzels are probably the best you'll get here, but what _is_ quinoa and is it really edible?

The worst rating – the Hollow Tummy

Homes with a high snackage quotient are an automatic yes if they ask you to babysit.

Homes with a medium snackage quotient are a possible yes, depending on other factors, like how bratty the kids are, whether they have cable TV, how desperately you want the money, that kind of thing.

Homes with a low snackage quotient are a probable no, but if there's something else really great about the family, you could still say yes. If they have a great DVD collection, if they have a hot tub you can use once the kids are asleep — those are good reasons to overlook the poor snackage.

you can always bring your own. →

Nacho fixin's all included along with ← some microwave popcorn and 3 kinds of cookies.

Emergency Snackage Kit

That made me wonder.
↓

# QUIZ #2

# WHAT MATTERS MOST WHEN YOU'RE BABYSITTING?

① Good snacks? Which of these is a deal breaker, meaning no babysitting, no way?

ⓐ Vegetarian food.

Here's a nice veggie tray.

Bleh!

ⓑ Health food.

There's soy milk if you're thirsty and gluten-free cookies with carob.

These are cookies?

ⓒ Gross food.

I made turkey surprise for dinner, so help yourself.

It sure is a surprise.

② The amount you're paid? How little are you willing to accept?

ⓐ The bare minimum.

This seems like a fair amount.

Fair to who? The other kid, the one who said no to babysitting?

ⓑ Being paid in trade.

We'll pay you with these nice old clothes.

They're not really old—they're vintage.

No—they're OLD!

ⓒ The oops, I forgot.

How embarrassing! I'm out of cash. We'll have to owe you for this one. Promise to pay you next time.

There's no next time until I get paid!

③ Easy kids? Where do you draw the line on difficult behavior?

④ Home entertainment? Do you need a big-screen TV or does a radio satisfy you? What's the least you'll accept?

If you answered mostly a's, you need a comfortable
situation for babysitting to be worth your while.
You'd rather be at home or out with friends than
face the smallest difficulties. ↑

*you shouldn't take any job dealing with customer service. Handling cranky people is NOT for you.*

If you answered mostly b's, you're
focused on your goals and don't let annoyance
get in the way of earning good money. You can
↗ babysit under less-than-ideal circumstances.

*I put myself here. Some things aren't worth any amount of money, but I'm not lazy.*

If you answered mostly c's, you like a challenge.
You might want to join the Peace Corps when
you're older or take the kind of job that offers
hazard pay — you're willing to face the nitty-gritty. ↗ *cute*
You could even babysit the Terrible Toroni Triplets.

*Or you could be a substitute teacher. You have a strong stomach for rude kids.*

MINE!

NO, MINE!

NO, MINE!

Definitely NOT mine!

*This is where Carly is. Nothing scares her. So what happens if I'm not up to her level? What if I can't take the Terrible Toroni Triplets?*

I gave Carly the test to see what mattered most to her. She said money, just as I expected. She can handle ANYTHING so long as she's paid enough.

I can deal with a brat, no problem. But it's got to be worth my while. The Reeses are an example of a perfect job because they pay well, they have a nice, comfortable home with good snacks, and the kids are easy.

I agree with Carly, except I'm sure there are some kids I wouldn't want to babysit no matter how much I was paid. What if I had to take care of Baby Cleo? Or imagine the mean Mr. L. as a toddler. Forget it!

Goo!

I bet she bit and scratched and screamed and stank and EVERYTHING you don't want in a baby! Plus she was Cleo - enough said!

Which made me think, how bratty does a kid have to be to make the money not worth it? And if a kid is really horrible, is there some amount of money that would make it bearable? I mean, everything has its price. Do I have a price?

BRAT RANGE FINDER
GREEN ZONE
YELLOW ZONE
RED ZONE
These kids are safe.
These kids can go either way – watch out!
These kids are terrors– NO WAY, NOT EVER! (Unless there's a VERY big pile of cash in exchange.)
Wants to play a game with you.
Wants to play a particular game with you and HAS to go first.
Wants to play a specific game, has to go first, has to win, and insists on playing over and over again.
We have to set up the game again!
You did it all wrong before!
Help! I'll go crazy!
Won't eat anything green, but eats pizza after picking off the onions.
Won't touch or eat anything green – you have to pick off the onions.
Won't eat or touch anything that ever had anything green on it. Has a tantrum demanding a new, pure pizza.
You're trying to poison me! You know I HATE green things. Get them out of my sight–NOW!!
Will gladly take a bath so long as you make it fun with tub toys.
Will take a bath if you promise a special treat afterward, like ice cream.
Wrestling a big crocodile would be easier than getting this kid into a bathtub – don't even try!
Get that kid away from me! Talk about scary!

It seems like everyone has a different range for tolerating brats. Carly's is high, but mine is pretty low. Does that make us a good or bad team? Carly thinks it doesn't matter because her being with me will make it easier for me to put up with nasty kids. I'm not so sure.

What if I disappoint Carly by making <u>her</u> deal with the brat?

What if she thinks I don't deserve half the money? Will that start a fight?

Suddenly babysitting reminded me of why I hate team sports — I'm always afraid I'll let the team down and they'll lose, all because of me.

What if being around me makes the bad kid act even worse? Will Carly blame me?

Can we be friends <u>and</u> business partners or will working together ruin our friendship?

I didn't tell Carly my worries because she says it's exhausting to reassure me when I'm like that, and it's a waste of time to worry about something that hasn't happened yet. But that's what worrying is — fretting over the future. Once it becomes the present, you don't worry — you react (sad, mad, relieved). Whatever it is, at least you're no longer worried. It's the unknown element, not being sure exactly what to expect, that makes me nervous. I feel like it's all a big gamble whether you deal with brats or not.

Babysitting Roulette — will you hit the jackpot or lose your shirt?

JACKPOT! Kid sleeps the whole time!

HORRORS! Kid is a brat and vomits on your legs.

MIXED BAG — Kid makes a big mess, but cleans it up after you nag.

GOOD — Kid needs a bit of attention but you have much —

YUUCHI! Kid is adorable but throws up all over — not cute!

BEARABLE — Kid is high energy and exhausting but sweet. Goes to bed late.

NIGHTMARE! Kid is a total monster — trashes house AND says you say —

GRAND PRIZE! Kid does every-thing you say — sweet AND —

Some of the bad stuff isn't even the kid's fault — it's just that I'm responsible for taking care of the mess. I can't leave it for the parent and still expect to get paid.

At dinner, Cleo kept on asking questions about the Reeses, like she couldn't believe Carly and me had it so easy. Was she trying to scare me about Saturday's job or was she just jealous? I definitely wasn't going to tell her about my worries. No matter what, I wanted Cleo to think I was totally in control and that babysitting was a snap for me. Even if I wasn't and it wasn't,

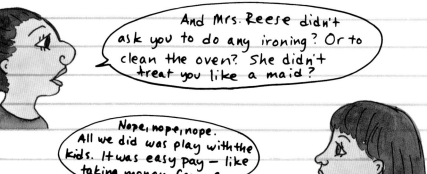

And Mrs. Reese didn't ask you to do any ironing? Or to clean the oven? She didn't treat you like a maid?

Nope, nope, nope. All we did was play with the kids. It was easy pay — like taking money from a baby.

That made Cleo really sore.

Sweet kids, nice parents - you lucked out.

Hope it's as good for you this Saturday.

← she didn't look like she hoped any such thing!

I know it'll be as good. What could go wrong? The kids will probably go to sleep around 8:00, so the last 4 hours Carly and I will be paid for watching TV. That's a good deal! And before that all we have to do is play games and read books. I've heard that some parents try to take advantage of babysitters and ask them to do stuff that has nothing to do with their kids – like ironing or oven cleaning – but the Reeses aren't like that. Cleo must be getting them confused with another family. Maybe the Fitches. Leah babysat for them once and they asked her to rake leaves and mow the lawn too.

Leah told me she's fine with washing dishes or cooking for kids, but there are some lines she absolutely won't cross. Cleo said she won't even wash dishes — that's what the dishwasher is for. The most she's willing to do is put the dirty plates in the machine!

# Extra Chores Tolerance Scale

Everyone is different! See where you fit on the scale!

**I'm fine making meals so long as they're zappable.**

low tolerance — will only do the least possible extra work. →

Microwaving is okay. Real cooking? No way! **1**

Real cooking is okay. Loading the dishwasher? Never! → **2**

I am, however, willing to pile dishes in the sink.

Loading the dishwasher is fine. Washing dishes by hand? I don't think so! → **3**

What? And chip my nail polish?

Washing dishes by hand is tolerated. Sorting and folding laundry is off-limits. → **4**

It's one thing to touch a dirty glass. It's another to touch clean underwear.

**5**

Sorting and folding laundry is doable. Ironing? Forget it! Who irons anymore anyway?

It's kind of soothing to fold warm clothes — and you can watch TV while doing it.

**6**

Ironing is okay, but I have no idea how to do it. Are you sure you want me to?

What's that funny mark on the shirt?

And why does it smell like something's burning?

**7**

I'm willing to iron, but I can't, so I'll scrub toilets instead.

This is for your own good, believe me!

**8**

Wait a second — no one is willing to scrub toilets! Even the most tolerant babysitter won't go that far. Everything but that!

High tolerance — you're willing to do it all, even my homework!

Eww! Just looking at a toilet brush is gross! You can't seriously expect me to touch it?!

If you're a 1-2 on the scale, you'll do the bare minimum. If you're a 3-4, you're willing to do a little extra. If you're a 5-6, can you come clean my room? If you're a 7-8, you can come clean my house!

I asked Carly to rate where she is on the Extra Chores Tolerance Scale to check if we're compatible. I'm willing to go as high as 6 — see, I don't mind hard work, just difficult people. I admit I have no idea how to iron, but I don't mind trying. Carly can iron, but she said she still wouldn't do it. I'm more tolerant of chores. She's more tolerant of brats.

I don't mind hard work, but I have my pride.

If you hire me to baby-sit, _that's_ what I'm doing, _not_ house-keeping!

And since we're working together, _you're_ not doing that stuff either! We need a standard to stick to.

"Okay," I agreed. "So what's our standard?"
"We'll do work that has to do with taking care of the kid, like making dinner and cleaning up afterward, but _no_ extra work. Not even something easy like dusting or taking out the trash. Those things aren't connected to babysitting."
I love that Carly's so clear about all this. She's right — we'll be great partners despite our differences.

It's a good thing we set our standards, because now we have ⛭2⛭ jobs lined up. Mrs. Silvano, a friend of Mrs. Reese, called today and asked if we could watch her baby tomorrow night. Her regular sitter canceled and Mrs. Reese recommended Carly and me. Cleo is FURIOUS.

I give you a couple of jobs and now you're stealing work from me.

What am I? Chopped liver? Don't I count?

Why didn't Mrs. Reese give Mrs. Silvano my name? I'm way more experienced than you!

I tried to calm her down.

"Probably because Mrs. Reese knows you won't change diapers — which isn't like washing dishes, you know. It's part of taking care of a kid."

"Suddenly YOU'RE the expert, telling me what I should do!" Cleo roared. "I'm GREAT with babies, even if I don't change diapers. I mean — GROSS!! They don't pay me enough for that. That deserves HIGH hazard pay. And who says a baby can't sit in its own juices for an hour or so? A little marinating never hurt anyone."

Hold you? NO WAY!

Goo!

P.U.! I could just imagine being around a stinky baby that long. You'd have to handle the kid with special tongs to keep the stench far away. →

Luckily for me, Carly says she'll handle any stink-bomb diapers. All I have to do is provide the expertise, since I have more experience with babies because of taking care of my half brother, George. That's more than Carly's done. She hasn't actually changed a diaper yet, so she has no idea what she's getting herself into. I sure do! And I know that babies aren't all the same—I've met George's baby buddies from day care.

## TYPES OF BABIES

There are many sub-categories, but these are the 4 basic types. Avoid the Screamer and you'll be fine.

I won't even go into the pacifier-addict type, since that's a subset of the Screamer. It's enough to say that with this kind of baby, a lost pacifier is the basis for WWIII—full screaming throttle.

The Screamer— easily recognizable by her bright red face. <u>Nothing</u> makes her happy. <u>Everything</u> enrages her. You're left feeling totally helpless.

← The Smiler - it's amazing how a happy baby puts everyone around in a good mood. Even changing diapers isn't too bad with this cutie.

The Sleeper - if you're → lazy, this is the baby for you. You don't have to do anything, just be there in case of emergency — like an urgent need to raid the fridge.

Will that Screamer ever shut up?

This is George's type →

The Energetic Mover — this baby ← can be a charmer but a lot of work. You'd be amazed how fast a baby can crawl! Good luck trying to change a diaper! You have to catch him first and then you need 6 hands for the job.

# TYPES OF TODDLERS

Babies grow into these 4 basic types — again, the Screamer is definitely the worst.

← The Screamer — screamer babies often grow up into screamer toddlers, which are even worse. They can have tantrums for no reason at all and once they begin, there's NO stopping them. You need real patience to babysit this kid or a good set of earplugs or be really, REALLY desperate for money.

The Smiler — these are sweet, irresistible toddlers. They're fun to be around even if they like to watch food fall on the floor or ask you to play catch over and over again. They're the kind of kid who asks what I call the endless question. (No matter what you answer, they'll ask another question until you finally say, like parents do, "BECAUSE!") →

*Bye, bye peas! Here come the noodles!*

*why is the sky blue? Why do we have 10 toes?*

*why is a ball round?*

↑
WARNING — Don't pick up whatever they throw and give it back because they'll just throw it again...and again... and AGAIN! Amusing for them, but not for you!

The Sleeper — toddlers don't sleep as much as babies, but if you're lucky, you'll have one who falls asleep right after dinner, leaving you free to watch TV.

George is growing into this. Babysitting him will <u>really</u> be work!

The only bad part is putting pajamas on a limp body — no easy task, but better than a thrashing, high-energy kid.

Look at me!

Don't move an inch!

The Energetic Mover —

even worse than the energetic baby because now she can walk and climb and pull stuff down and get into some real tricky spots. WATCH OUT! If you look away for a minute, the kid can be out the door and in the street before you know it!

Let's play statue. You're it — now be still as a statue!

I showed Carly the baby and toddler types and she was impressed.

"Let's hope the Silvano baby is a sleeper," she said.

"If she's a screamer, we could call Cleo and let her take over," I suggested.

"No way!" Carly said. "I'm not going to be beaten by a baby!" I didn't say anything, but I know how horrible a difficult baby can be. She may be smaller than you and not know how to talk, but the power of her screaming can make the strongest grown-up feel completely powerless.

Please stop crying! I'll do anything! PLEASE!

WAAAH!

And a toddler having a temper tantrum? Forget it! There's no calming that storm. You practically need riot gear once he starts throwing cups, toys, food, anything he can reach.

Godzilla toddler, leaving a path of destruction behind her.

So I was a little worried about the Silvano baby. Carly and I got to the house early — me because I was nervous, Carly because she was eager. It turned out to be a good thing, since Mrs. Silvano had a <u>lot</u> of instructions. I felt like I should be taking notes.

She's a very easy baby, but if she fusses, walk around with her. And sing to her — that usually works. Or you can try rocking her for a while or

Make sure her bottle is warm, but <u>not</u> hot, and there's some rice cereal if she's still hungry. If the house gets too cold, the thermostat is in the front hall, but don't set it above 7

It all seemed like basic stuff we already knew anyway (or was easy to figure out), so I don't get why she bothered to give us so many details. She acted like she was handing over a delicate electronic device with a 500-page instruction manual instead of a simple baby. I mean, all a baby does is cry, eat, poop, and sleep. How complicated is that?

Then she kept on saying she was going to leave, but there was always one last thing she had to say. Finally, after doing that 6 times, she really did leave.

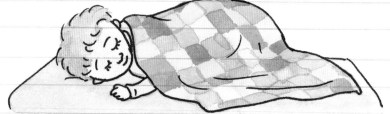

After all that, the baby slept the whole time her mom was gone. Maybe she was exhausted by all the instructions. I know Carly and I were pretty tired of the walking, talking user's guide.

We ended up playing cards. It was a totally easy job. I mean, the babysitting part was easy. Dealing with Mrs. Silvano was another story. And I didn't get a chance to show Carly how good I am with babies. I wanted to impress her. I hope I get another chance.

We're so lucky! she's still asleep.

Yeah. We don't even have to change a diaper.

Maybe Carly was right — I worried too much over nothing.

I didn't get to show off my baby expertise, so I made some new guide pages instead. I knew Carly would love them.

## TYPES OF PARENTS

Just like babies and kids fit into several categories, so do parents.

> Our little darling never makes messes.

> She cleans up after herself all the time! You'll see.

> She's a real angel!

Doters - these parents think their kid can do no wrong, which is fine if their kid is a Smiler or a Sleeper. Otherwise, watch out! You'll get blamed for everything!

> If my parents come home and find this mess, you're in trouble! They know their little sweetiekins NEVER makes a mess, so it's all your fault.

> Maybe it's time your parents learned what an "angel" you really are! I'm not picking up after you.

Believe me, this tactic won't work. No matter how much proof you have, the parents will be mad at you, not their kid. You can't change that!

Rule-bound — these parents are like certain teachers. They have looooong lists of rules and there's no way you can keep them all. These parents are never satisfied, no matter how clean you leave the house or how long their kid's been asleep by the time they come home. Nothing you do is enough.

If it's exhausting for you, think of what it's like for the poor kid! →

We keep the rules posted on the refrigerator. Make sure you read them all. Play time lasts exactly 20 minutes. Then it's time for something educational — it could be reading, math games, or listening to Mozart. Remember, no snacks before dinner and, of course, no dessert until every vegetable is eaten. Make sure teeth are thoroughly...

Generous — these parents are the best. They aren't too demanding and they know how to make a babysitter feel welcome. In fact, they know how to make babysitting feel like a mini-vacation.

Help yourself to whatever you want in the kitchen. We ordered a pizza for dinner and there are plenty of snacks. Once Callie is asleep, you're welcome to use our hot tub — it's very relaxing.

Nervous — these parents are kind of like the rule-bound ones, but with an added anxious edge. They're the ones who constantly call to check up on how their kid is doing. Or they have problems leaving, like Mrs. Silvano. They can't quite trust you to babysit.

He's fine — just like he was 5 minutes ago.

And 5 minutes before that.

No, he isn't running with scissors. He didn't drown in the bathtub. He didn't choke on his dinner. HE'S FINE!!!

Taskmasters — these parents think babysitting is a cushy, easy job and they're not getting their money's worth unless you do other work for them. Either be clear about what you're willing to do or be prepared to work your tail off.

Here's the mop for scrubbing the floor. Don't forget the laundry and clean the oven too.

Am I a babysitter or a slave?

I'm getting better with little kids and their parents, at least in this guide (where I'm storing up experience). But I still have the most experience with babies, so I made this quiz for Carly to see where she fits on the range of babysitters from Cleo to me. (Although I already know she's NOT like Cleo!)

## QUIZ #3

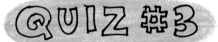

# WHAT KIND OF BABYSITTER ARE YOU?
(for babies, not older kids)

| ① What do you like to do with little babies? | | | |
|---|---|---|---|
| ⓐ Play peek-a-boo and talk baby talk. | ⓑ Cuddle them. | ⓒ Watch them sleep. | ⓓ Nothing. |

④ What's the perfect temperature for a baby's bottle?
ⓐ Exactly 81.5°.
ⓑ Not too hot, not too cold, just right.
ⓒ Refreshingly cold – adding ice cubes helps.
ⓓ Whatever it is – babies aren't picky.
Good thing I brought my handy-dandy thermometer!
Just the way Baby Bear likes it, right?
Now there's a drink!
I'm sure they left it in the freezer for a reason.
C'mon, baby, have your milk popsicle!

⑤ What's the perfect food for a baby?
ⓐ Whatever you can clean up easily.
ⓑ Whatever you can mush or strain.
ⓒ Whatever you can get them to eat.
ⓓ Pizza!
The most important thing is to have the baby wear a bib.
And NO food throwing is allowed.
It's a baby feast – avocado, applesauce, and rice cereal!
I've tried EVERYTHING! What will you eat?!
Well, if you don't want it, that means more for me.
Go ahead, gum it down!
?

If you answered mostly a's, you're careful and fastidious, neat and clean. You're fine with babies, but you're even better organizing closets — just like Leah.

Leah's a talented artist, a loyal friend, and a neat freak.

If you answered mostly b's, you're warm and friendly and get along well with babies. If you had a friend with you, then everything would be perfect. You're like me!

Carly said b's, like me — does that mean she doesn't need me?

If you answered mostly c's, you're practical but more interested in your own comfort than the baby's. Another job might fit you better. You're like Gigi.

Gigi is Cleo's best friend. She's very stylish and elegant — which is good in itself, but not good for babysitting. She's too worried about chipping her nails to take great care of a baby.

If you answered mostly d's, you're too selfish to be a good babysitter. You need to think about the kid every now and then, not just stuffing your face. You're like my sister, Cleo.

Hey, my only problem is I don't do diapers. Big deal!

When Cleo heard that we didn't even have to change a diaper at the Silvanos, she was madder than ever.

It's not fair! You've had 2 easy jobs in a row. Babysitting isn't like that, you know. There are brats out there. And crazy parents.

I told her Mrs. Silvano wasn't exactly easy, but I had to admit she wasn't horrible, either. She just talked too much. That kind of thing is easy to ignore, especially when there's money at the end of the day.

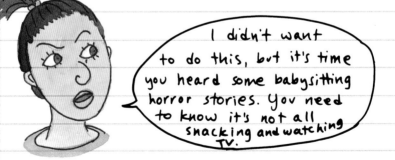

I didn't want to do this, but it's time you heard some babysitting horror stories. You need to know it's not all snacking and watching TV.

She didn't sound at all like she didn't want to do it. She looked thrilled to tell us a whole collection of Babysitting-Gone-Bad stories, things that happened to other kids, not just her.

I'm putting the best two in this guide.

## Story #1:

## Embarrassing Moments

(Naturally this is Cleo's story, told in her own words.)

*Ahem, let me begin.*

"I've never had a problem with kids. Despite what Amelia says, little kids LOVE me! And parents do too — really! I'm an expert, a pro, a natural babysitter."

"But everyone makes mistakes, right? We're all human, aren't we? Anyway, there was this one time I was babysitting Deke, a kid I'd babysat many times before. Since he was such an easy kid and I knew he went to bed early, I thought it would be okay to have my boyfriend come over. I mean, it's boring by yourself. And Deke's parents never said I couldn't have a friend over. Okay, I didn't ask, I admit that, but like I said, they'd never given me a rule against having friends visit. So Corey came over."

This is Corey (artist's rendition).

*Corey? Who's Corey? Corey?!*

*What do boys see in her? I don't get it.*

*Cleo's had more boyfriends than I can keep track of. How? Why?*

"And ya know, we were getting comfortable because Deke was sound asleep. That kid is sweet, never a problem. So it was cool with Corey and me EXCEPT Deke's parents came home earlier than they said they would. It was pretty embarrassing — for them more than for me."

"Well, actually for Corey — he sure turned red!"

↑
Cleo wasn't sure who was more upset — Deke's parents or Corey.

↑
Cleo was fine, of course. Nothing embarrasses <u>her</u>.

"The end of the story is that Corey's not my boyfriend anymore (no loss there) and I haven't babysat for Deke since then."

So there's Cleo's story in her own words (with my pictures). Somehow I don't think I'll ever have the same problem. And anyway, the baby wasn't horrible — Cleo was!

# Story #2 : Difficult Moments

(This one is Gigi's.)

Gigi is Cleo's best friend, which you would think means she has terrible taste, but really she doesn't (except in her choice of best friend). She used to babysit a lot, but now she doesn't, all because of her WORST night ever.

What's really surprising about this story is that normally I don't have ANY trouble babysitting — kids listen to me. So do their parents. I'm not the kind of person you mess with. Most little kids sense that. Not this one.

I'll let Gigi tell the story:

"I'm good at handling kids. They respect me and I respect them. Even bratty kids behave around me — or else! I have the magic touch. Or so I thought until I babysat for the Shrieking Terror."

"I would _never_ have said yes if I'd known how difficult this kid was, but as long as her parents were there, she was a perfect little angel."

"The second they drove away, she started to shriek. Just like that!"

She looks innocent, but looks mean nothing!

WARNING: CONTINUED EXPOSURE TO THIS KID MAY BE HAZARDOUS TO YOUR HEALTH AND SANITY. TAKE ALL PRECAUTIONS!!

I didn't know mouths could open *that* wide! →

She was like a fire alarm going off – shrill, loud, grating, UNBEARABLE! ←

"One minute she's smiling and waving, the next she's yelling her head off."

"I tried EVERYTHING to shut her up! I offered to play a game, read a book, go to the park, draw pictures, bake cookies — nothing got through to her. She kept on screaming. I thought she'd shriek herself hoarse after an hour, but nope, she could go on forever. But _I_ couldn't. I'd had it! So I called her parents and said I couldn't stay. They could hear the screaming in the background and they begged me not to give up. They said if they came home early, they'd be rewarding her bad behavior. I said maybe, but if they didn't, they'd be punishing _me_."

"So they offered to pay me TRIPLE my regular rate if I would hold out for just one more hour. I should have said no — NOTHING was worth another hour with the Screaming Meanie — but I said yes. I'm tough. I figured I could take it."

But I couldn't... →

Either my head would explode or the kid would. It had better be the kid! ←

"I picked up the Shrieking Terror, carried her, kicking and screaming, to her room, and shut the door. Then I turned the TV on really loud. It wasn't so bad that way. I watched a cop show with a lot of explosions and her yells blended right in."

"When the parents came home, she was _still_ shrieking (but not _as_ loud — she did get tired after all). I took the money and told them never to call me again. They haven't."

SHRIEKING TERROR
NOT WANTED:

DO NOT BABYSIT THIS KID! LOOKS SWEET AND NICE — IS NOT!!

"Now their kid is on my banned list. None of my friends will ← ever babysit her either."

I have to admit, I admire how Gigi handled this. I would have thought it was all my fault, that something was really wrong with the kid, that she was hurt or scared or _something_. And I had to fix it.

Luckily this is a very rare thing to happen. Kids can be a little bratty, but usually not _this_ bad.' I know Cleo wanted to scare me with this story, but we've been lucky so far playing Babysitting Roulette. And we'll never have Cleo's problem either!

"Nice try, Cleo," I said, "but the third time's the charm. I bet our 3rd babysitting job will be the best of all!" Actually, I didn't see how it could get any easier, but we _would_ be making more money, lots more money.

I told Carly about Cleo's warnings and horror stories, but she just laughed.

"We know these kids, remember?" she said. "This isn't a game of Babysitting Roulette."

"Right," I agreed. "And we know the parents. They aren't a problem either."

"Plus we know what good snacks they have," Carly said.

"And cable TV," I added. "It's going to be a great Saturday!"

That's tomorrow. I can't wait until tomorrow night when I'll be rich, rich, RICH!

I would say I slept like a baby, except I had strange dreams of babysitting baby Cleo - yucch!

In my dream, Cleo looked exactly the same only she was a baby and she would NOT stop crying. Carly and I started screaming at each other because neither of us wanted to deal with her. We were all screaming.

We weren't being good partners. We were terrible. But it wasn't our fault — it was Cleo's. If she hadn't been such a brat, we would have been fine. That didn't stop us from yelling at each other, though. The dream ended when Carly finally grabbed Cleo, tucked her under her arm, and stomped off.

I was *so* relieved to wake up, I wanted to forget all about my bad dream. Carly and I *are* a good team and everything would be fine. At least, that's what I told myself.

That morning when we got to the Reeses' house, it was completely different from the last time we were there, just a few days ago. For a minute I thought I was still stuck in my nightmare— everyone was cranky and grumpy.

WAAAH!

NO! STOP! DON'T!

Tyler was crying because he spilled milk on his pajamas and he didn't want to change them.

Ruthy was mad because her mom was trying to brush her tangly hair.

Mr. Reese was yelling at everyone to behave and be quiet, they had to go.

That's enough, kids! We're leaving. Amelia and Carly will help you out.

Mrs. Reese was embarrassed by it all.

Sorry, girls, to rush off like this. I'm sure things will calm down as soon as we leave.

Only they didn't. Calm down, that is. It was a bad start to a bad day and things just got worse.

It took 20 minutes to convince Tyler to change out of his milky pajamas, and as soon as he did, he spilled orange juice all over his shirt. That meant another 20 minutes of begging and pleading until he was in clean clothes. Carly wanted to be sure there would be no more messes.

This time if you're going to eat or drink anything, you're wearing a garbage bag first!

She meant like a kind of giant bib, not that Tyler belonged in the trash.

But somehow what she said made an even bigger mess.

WAAAH! You're mean! You want to throw me away! You think I'm garbage!

I'll show you! I'm running away! You'll never catch me! Run, run, as fast as you can. You can't catch me! I'm speedy man!

While Carly was chasing after Tyler — he was surprisingly fast, just like he said — Ruthy was trying some fast moves of her own on me.

Since I brushed my hair like a big girl, I get my big-girl reward.

Mom always makes me a chocolate sundae and lets me watch a movie after I brush my hair. It's my big-girl hair prize.

Big goo-goo innocent eyes made me extra suspicious.

It seemed like making a really big deal out of a little wispy brushed hair, and I had the feeling Ruthy was lying. But I wasn't sure. So I made her the sundae and let her pick out a movie to watch. At least she wasn't running through the house and climbing the furniture the way Tyler was.

Carly finally tackled Tyler and told him for the 100th time she wasn't going to throw him into the garbage.

"Tell you what," she said, glaring at me. "Amelia will make you a nice chocolate sundae for breakfast like she made your sister and you can both watch a movie."

Was Carly annoyed at me because I didn't help her chase Tyler or because I made the sundae for Ruthy?

"I'm just trying to smooth things out around here," I said. "What's the big deal?"

"I don't think ice cream is the way to solve bad behavior." Carly's voice was colder than the mint chocolate chip.

"Okay, partner," I said. "Then you solve it." I headed toward the living room.

"Wait!" Carly called. "I'm sorry — we shouldn't fight. We have to work together." She started scooping ice cream into a bowl.

"Yay!" Tyler yelled. "Ice cream, ice cream, ice cream!"

"You certainly are screaming," I said.

Carly looked at me and laughed. Just like that we were friends and partners again.

We had to team up. We had to work together. Otherwise, things would melt down completely.

Tyler was happy with his sundae, but Ruthy wasn't. "That's not fair!" she wailed. "You only get ice cream if you brush your hair. Tyler didn't brush his hair!"

"You liar!" Tyler yelled. "You made that whole thing up to get a sundae."

"You're the liar!" Ruthy raged. She ran up to Tyler and kicked him.

"Stop it, both of you, NOW!" I grabbed Ruthy. Carly grabbed Tyler. It wasn't even 8 a.m. yet and I was exhausted. So was Carly. Unfortunately the kids had plenty of energy.

So we resorted to the time-honored, last-ditch resort of all babysitters (including parents). We parked them in front of the TV.

That gave us an hour of peace while we cleaned up the kitchen.

"I'm sorry I snapped at you like that," Carly said. "The most important thing is to work together, no matter what. Even if I don't like what you're doing."

"Even if," I agreed. "Especially if! We're going to handle things differently, okay?"

Carly nodded. Then the movie ended and our reprieve was over. It wasn't even 10 a.m. and Ruthy wanted lunch.

There she was with those big, begging eyes again. →

My tummy's hungry. Can I make a sandwich? Pleeeease! Mommy always lets me.

I didn't want her fooling me again, so I asked Tyler if it was true about the sandwiches. If I had to face another mess in the kitchen, there had to be a real reason.

oh, yes. _Whenever_ we're hungry, we're allowed to make sandwiches. Any time of day. Mommy says that's better than snacking on cookies or chips.

He had big, innocent eyes too.

but what he said made sense. And since they'd had ice cream for breakfast, a sandwich sounded like a good thing, or at least a healthier one.

So I told Ruthy she could make a sandwich and naturally Tyler wanted to make one now too. It became a contest between them who could come up with the most original sandwich.

Ruthy's

← mayo
← sardines
← pickles
← left-over french fries
← baloney
← relish
← marshmallows
← cold toaster waffle
← cold hot dog
← salad dressing
ketchup

← mayo

Tyler's

honey
pickles
cream cheese
salami
mustard
lime jello
chili beans

cold spaghetti
ketchup
tofu

peanut butter →

It kept them busy, but the kitchen was a horrible mess again. The sandwiches themselves were a mess.

"Those are gross!" I said. "You're not really going to eat them, are you?"

"Of course not," said Tyler. "That would be rude. We made them for you and Carly."

Carly tried not to gag. "How sweet of you," she said. "I'm sorry I can't eat mine since I'm allergic to pickles, but I'm sure Amelia will love hers."

"Thanks a _lot_," I whispered to her.

Tyler and Ruthy looked at me with their big, big eyes.

I couldn't. Really. No matter how big their eyes were or how much I hurt their feelings.

I decided to make my eyes as big as theirs.

you guys are SO sweet! These sandwiches are so, SO special, I want to save them and bring them home, so I can give one to my sister, Cleo.

That idea was a big success. They were so excited that Cleo would get one of their sandwiches, they even added an extra layer of grape jelly and peanut butter. Yum!

Unfortunately when it was really lunchtime, they refused to eat anything. Until we let them make toasted peanut butter and jelly sandwiches, which naturally meant getting sticky peanut butter and jelly all over the oven, table, chairs, floor, and walls. Carly even got some in her hair. I stepped in some. We may have been working as a team, but this day was really not going well. Every hour seemed to last 3 hours. I didn't see how we could survive until 8 p.m., when the kids would finally go to bed.

tick

tock

tock

tick

I thought watching the clock at school was agony.

Every time we got the kitchen clean, it was gunked up again. I wondered if this would be our babysitting horror story.

I thought nothing could move slower than those hands. I was wrong. The kitchen clock at the Reeses was _much_ slower. Time was practically standing still. Why do fun things feel like they happen so quickly and terrible things plod along at a snail's pace to make them even _worse_?

Between lunch and dinner we had 2 accidents, 4 messes, and one major disaster. Carly lost her temper twice and I lost mine so many times, I was sure I'd never find it again. This wasn't anywhere near the fun time we'd planned.

Mess #1: (I'm not even counting the kitchen messes.) Ruthy decided to play dress-up and took EVERYTHING out of her mom's closet (including

slip as bridal veil →

some stuff I'm sure Mrs. Reese didn't want anyone seeing, like thong underwear).

Mom's makeup smeared all over her face. →

lace blouse as wedding gown →

clomping around in expensive high heels ←

Mess #2: Before we could stop her, Ruthy chewed up 2 lipsticks, muddied up 3 colors of eyeshadow, and dropped a mascara wand down the toilet.

Mess #3: Tyler was busy all this time in the garage. He spilled oil, paint, and sawdust all over, including on himself. He needed to change AGAIN and take a bath, which led to the major disaster.

Seeing the mess in the garage made Carly lose her temper for the first time. She'd been amazingly calm with Ruthy's stuff. With Tyler, she snapped.
↓

What were you thinking?!

This stuff is DANGEROUS!! It's not for little kids, so don't tell me your parents let you do this! Tell the TRUTH!

Tyler looked sorry, very sorry.
↙

"No, they don't," he admitted. "But I wanted to surprise them with a cool invention. Only it didn't work."

← The only thing he invented was a gunky, smelly, hard-to-clean up mess.

I wasn't sure how to do it, but I started to clean up the garage while Carly turned on the water for a bath. It was a good thing there were two of us. I couldn't imagine dealing with these kids by myself. I wondered, how did Cleo do it? Was this why she'd warned us so much?

I couldn't wash away the oil stain, but I did the best I could. I felt like I'd been scrubbing things all day. Wait – that's because I _had_! When I slumped back into the house, Ruthy ran up to me, all excited.

"Look!" she yelled, pointing to the bathroom. Water was running down the hallway, flooding into the bedrooms. I sloshed through it to the bathroom. The bathtub was overflowing!

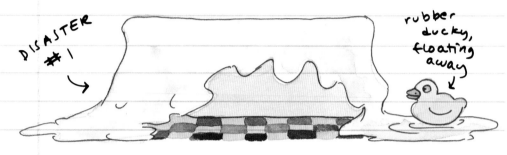

DISASTER #1 →

rubber ducky, floating away ↙

I turned off the tap and opened up the drain, but there was still water all over the floors. And where was Carly? I didn't have time to look for her — I grabbed every towel I could find to sop up all the water. I had to use all the towels in the house, even the washcloths and paper towels. By the time I was finished, my pants, socks, and shoes were soaked. And still no sign of Carly. Or Tyler.

"They must be outside," Ruthy said. "Tyler didn't want to take a bath, so he climbed the tree in the front yard. Carly went to get him down."

← towels, towels everywhere ↗

I couldn't face ANY more messes, so I took Ruthy with me and we both went outside to see what was going on.

Carly was just climbing down from the tree when we got there. Tyler was already on the ground. So were several snapped-off tree branches — mess #4 to clean up.

"You could have helped me!" Carly wailed. That was the second time she lost her temper. She was really mad, this time at me. "Look what happened!"

I looked. She'd scratched her face on a branch and tore her shirt. That was accident #1.

"I'm sorry," I said, "But look at _me_!"

My wet pants were dripping and my shoes made squishy sounds when ⟶ I walked.

"Oh no!" Carly groaned. "I forgot I left the water running!"

"Yes, you did." But I wasn't mad. I was relieved it was Carly's mistake, not mine.

"How bad is it?" she asked, not angry either anymore.

"Bad," I said. "A total disaster. But I've mopped up the water. Now we have a huge load of towels to wash."

I started a new bath for Tyler, keeping both kids with me, while Carly did the laundry, including my jeans and socks. I felt dumb sitting there in Mrs. Reese's way-too-big sweatpants, but I wasn't going to hang around in my underwear — that would have been disaster #2.

No way was I leaving the tub until Tyler got in _and_ out of it, all clean. I made Ruthy stay with us and we played I Spy, which is hard to do in a bathroom, where there's not much stuff.

For all the messes and mistakes, I felt strangely calm. Maybe because the worst had happened, but it wasn't my fault, and Carly wasn't any better at handling the problems than I was.

Unfortunately for Tyler, there were no towels to dry him with, so I used one of Mr. Reese's sweatshirts. Not as good as a towel, but better than nothing.

Finally, finally, finally, everyone and everything was clean. All I had to do was wait for my clothes and shoes to dry.

Then it was time for dinner. I couldn't take another mess.

Neither could Carly. Luckily we found a frozen pizza, something easy to make. And Ruthy and Tyler said they'd actually eat it, another bonus. So nothing bad happened until after dinner, when I stepped on one of Tyler's robot toys he'd left on the floor.

Me, hopping up and down on one foot, in pain.

That was accident #2. Now Carly and I both had Band-Aids. We really were well-matched partners, even in wounds.

not-so-innocent toy - all sharp edges

I'm lucky I didn't trip on the way-too-big sweat pants. Nothing like falling flat on your face to bring a day to a perfect end.

At 8 p.m. Ruthy and Tyler used their big, big eyes again and told us they were allowed to stay up until 9 p.m. But Carly and I were WAY beyond believing anything they said. We were <u>experienced</u> babysitters now (I mean, we'd experienced it <u>all</u>, as bad as it could get). We had those kids in bed at 8:05 and the lights out by 8:30.

After 13½ horrible hours, we could finally relax!

We sat on the sofa in a stupor.

"Is it really over?" Carly asked after a while.
"Are we done now?"

"Oh, we're done, all right," I said. "The question
is, will we ever do this again?"

"Was it really that bad?" Carly touched the
scratch on her face. "Think of all the money we're making."

I thought of it. Was it worth it? I wasn't sure,
but I did know one thing — if I babysit again, it
won't be like this. I'll do things differently. I won't
fall for stupid tricks kids try to play on me.

Then I started to laugh. I told Carly I was remembering
all the tricks I'd played on my babysitters. I guess we're even
now.

# Babysitting Tricks

I KNEW AND LOVED AND PLAYED ON
POOR, UNSUSPECTING BABYSITTERS!

Making up my own rules and saying they were Mom's.

I'm always allowed to sit this close.

Sweet, innocent eyes — yes, I used the goo-goo eye trick too.

mom says ice cream is a very nutritious meal.

I go to bed at 8:00, but I can read as long as I like.

Playing my own version of hide-n-seek.

Sneaking surprises under pillows — oh, that's where the peanut butter sandwich went!

Hiding books in the dishwasher — always check before turning on to avoid soggy pages!

Putting strange objects in the babysitter's shoe— plastic dinosaurs are especially painful and snails are especially gross!

Carly started laughing too. She had her own list of tricks she'd played. We both felt much better.

"You know," I said. "I was really worried that I'd let you down, not be a good partner, and you'd dump me — from the business and as a friend. Things were bad today, but that didn't happen."

"No, it didn't," Carly agreed. "We both made dumb mistakes, but we also helped each other." She grinned at me. "I couldn't have survived it without you, partner."

"Me neither, partner."

By the time the Reeses got home, I had my own dry clothes back on, and Carly and I had just finished watching a movie.

"How were the kids?" Mrs. Reese asked. "I hope they behaved."

Carly and I looked at each other.

"Oh, they did," I said.

"They went to bed right on time," Carly added.

"Great," said Mr. Reese. "Any chance you're free again next Saturday, same time, same place?"

We didn't even hesitate. We said it together, like the partners we are.

Of course!

And do we have a story to tell Cleo!

# Back-to-School Check List

Make sure you have:

- ☑ friends to walk to school with

- ☑ friends in your class

- ☑ friends to eat lunch with

- ☑ friends to help you with your homework

Don't go back to school without them!
And if you're new in school, make NEW friends!

↓                    ↓

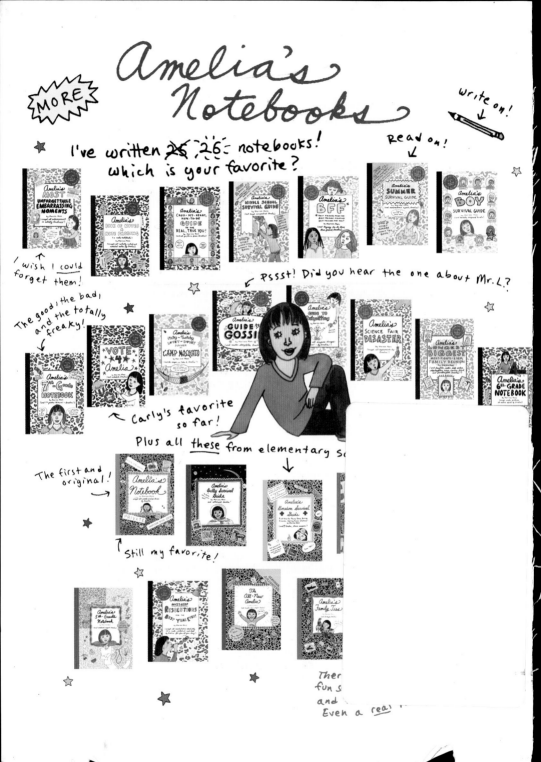

# Amelia's Notebooks

MORE

write on! ↓

★ I've written 25 26 notebooks! which is your favorite?

Read on! ↓

I wish I could forget them!

Pssst! Did you hear the one about Mr. L?

The good, the bad, and the totally freaky!

← Carly's favorite so far!

Plus all these from elementary s...

The first and original! →

↑ Still my favorite!

Ther... fun s... and... Even a rea...